THE
TIME MACHINE

H. G. WELLS

With an Introduction by
Greg Bear
and a New Afterword by
Simon J. James

SIGNET CLASSICS

SIGNET CLASSICS
Published by the Penguin Group
Penguin Group (USA) LLC, 375 Hudson Street,
New York, New York 10014

USA | Canada | UK | Ireland | Australia | New Zealand | India | South Africa | China
penguin.com
A Penguin Random House Company

Published by Signet Classics, an imprint of New American Library,
a division of Penguin Group (USA) LLC

First Signet Classics Printing, October 2002
First Signet Classics Printing (James Afterword), November 2014

Introduction copyright © Greg Bear, 2002
Afterword copyright © Simon J. James, 2014

Ⓒ REGISTERED TRADEMARK—MARCA REGISTRADA

ISBN 978-0-451-47070-6

Printed in the United States of America
10 9 8

Herbert George Wells was born in Bromley, Kent, England, on September 21, 1866. His father was a professional cricketer and sometime shopkeeper, his mother a former lady's maid. Although "Bertie" left school at fourteen to become a draper's apprentice (a life he detested), he later won a scholarship to the Normal School of Science in London, where he studied with the famous Thomas Henry Huxley. He began to sell articles and short stories regularly in 1893. In 1895, his immediately successful novel *The Time Machine* rescued him from a life of penury on a schoolteacher's salary. His other "scientific romances"—*The Island of Doctor Moreau* (1896), *The Invisible Man* (1897), *The War of the Worlds* (1898), *The First Men in the Moon* (1901), and *The War in the Air* (1908)—won him distinction as the father of science fiction. Henry James saw in Wells the most gifted writer of the age, but Wells, having coined the phrase "the war that will end war" to describe World War I, became increasingly disillusioned and focused his attention on educating mankind with his bestselling *Outline of History* (1920) and his later utopian works. Living until 1946, Wells witnessed a world more terrible than any of his imaginative visions, and he bitterly observed: "Reality has taken a leaf from my book and set itself to supercede me."

Greg Bear's novels and stories have appeared in more than twenty languages worldwide and have won numerous prizes, including two Hugos, five Nebulas, and the Prix Apollo. His novels include *Darwin's Radio* (winner of the Nebula and Endeavor awards), *Darwin's Children*, *Vitals*, *Blood Music*, *Eon*, *Queen of Angeles*, and *Moving Mars*. He has served as a consultant and a lecturer on space and defense policy, biotechnology and bioterrorism, multimedia entertainment, and Internet issues.

Simon J. James is Professor of Victorian Literature in the Department of English Studies, Durham University. He is the editor of *The Wellsian,* the peer-reviewed scholarly journal of the H. G. Wells Society. He has edited four H. G. Wells novels for Penguin Classics, as well as George Gissing's *Charles Dickens: A Critical Study*. James is the author of *Maps of Utopia: H. G. Wells, Modernity and the End of Culture* and *Unsettled Accounts: Money and Narrative Form in the Novels of George Gissing*.

Contents

Introduction   vii

The Time Machine   1

Appendix   109

Afterword   119

Selected Bibliogaphy   129

Introduction

BEFORE AIRPLANES, SPACE travel, and atomic
energy, before freeways and traffic jams, poison gas
and tanks, and just before the dawn of the twentieth
century, a nameless inventor in London discovered a
way to travel in time, using a mysterious machine assembled in a small private shop.

And an unknown journalist named Herbert George
Wells (1866–1946) leaped in a few short years to fame
and fortune.

If this is the first time you've read *The Time Machine,* then stop right here. Skip over this introduction,
for now, and get right to the story. When you're done,
if you wish, come back and join the discussion. It's
bound to be heated.

To this day, H. G. Wells is controversial, and I
doubt he would have had it any other way!

Welcome back. Now how do you feel about time
travel? Perplexed, skeptical, excited, a little sad?

By 1895, when *The Time Machine* was first published in book form, H. G. Wells had lived through
years of ill health, married and parted, and tried on a
career of teaching, then moved on to journalism and
writing reviews. He did not seem very successful at
anything, but he was enormously intelligent and ambi-

tious. And he knew he had one story, one idea, one
card up his sleeve that could possibly trump all of his
disadvantages.

A man, traveling in time, using a machine.

A Time Traveller.

Judging from many drafts and redrafts over at least
seven years, Wells knew that he had something big—
something that could launch his career very nicely indeed, if he only got it right.

He finally got it right. After its serialization in William Ernest Henley's *The New Review* in early 1895,
The Time Machine became a sensation. In an age in-
trigued by all the possibilities of science and mathe-
matics, Wells's first work of fiction was like a brisk
slap in the face. The future will be marvelous, the
young Wells told his audience—and also tragic, even
horrible. All things biological must end, or give way
to new forms, he suggested, following the dour lead
of his most influential teacher, Darwin's "Bulldog,"
T. H. Huxley.

For Victorian England, the picture of humanity di-
vided into the diminutive, weak, and sun-dwelling Eloi
and those technological dwellers in underground darkness, the Morlocks, must have seemed particularly
grotesque—mirroring as it did the tottering class system: quite literally, Upstairs and Downstairs.

In this bleak picture of distant futurity, Wells gives us
a final glimmer of human love, innocent and childlike,
in the outstretched hand of the tiny Eloi Weena . . . love,
however, too weak to withstand the brutal forces of evolution and necessity, and far too swiftly destroyed. As a
final fillip, Wells shows us that eventually even the necessity of biological evolution will give way, as the sun
swells and reddens, life reverts to the crustacean and
then to the (possibly) molluscan or protozoan, and the
Earth finally freezes over.

It is an utterly chilling message, mixing as it does human sentiment, contemporary scientific knowledge, unwavering pessimism, and a sense of cosmic wonder and discovery, with the realization of the limited condition of the human race. As a novelistic tour de force, nothing like it had ever been published.

Coming on the heels of decades of speculation about both evolution and geometry, and bringing together recent theories in astronomy and geology, *The Time Machine* hit the Victorian intellect squarely between the eyes. It was the first modern science fiction novel.

Within nine years, H. G. Wells would write seven more novels—*The Island of Doctor Moreau* (1896), *The Invisible Man* (1897), *The War of the Worlds* (1898), *When the Sleeper Wakes* (1899), *The First Men in the Moon* (1901), *The Food of the Gods* (1904), *In the Days of the Comet* (1906)—and numerous short stories that would shape and define twentieth-century science fiction. By 1914 and the beginning of World War I, Wells was one of the bestselling authors in the English language.

He became the twentieth-century prototype of the angry young man, brilliant and full of contradictions. Throughout his life, Wells promoted his changeable brand of socialism yet toyed with (early on, at least) a belief in God, called for equality of the sexes yet was a flagrant womanizer, decried class distinctions yet sought the approval of the rich, the powerful, and the famous—and then, just as quickly, denounced them!

In the 1920s, his *Outline of History* would sell millions of copies. He would become so famous and so influential that authors seeking a reputation—or at least some intellectual balance—would cock their hats and shy stones at his overwhelming success and his pugnacious attitudes.

C. S. Lewis parodied Wells's brand of evolution and rationalism from a theist perspective in his science fiction novels *Out of the Silent Planet, Perelandra,* and *That Hideous Strength*. Lewis built an intellectually confused, villainous character named Weston on the frame of a number of scientific acquaintances, possibly including J.B.S. Haldane and Wells. Even as late as 1955, William Golding would reply to Wells's portrait (in *An Outline of History*) of low, bestial Neanderthals with his own depiction of them as scions of a kinder nature, brutalized by modern humans, in *The Inheritors*.

Wells was a marvelous sounding board, and there's evidence he enjoyed this kind of hurly-burly. What he did not enjoy was a bad review or being ignored.

Above all, he hated being ignored.

All of Wells's early scientific romances are accessible to a person of average education. They are clearly and elegantly written, not very heavy on the character bits (but convincing in what is shown), realistic despite their fantastic elements, clear-eyed about animal nature—and highly imaginative. They are also thoroughly satirical, though often written with a straight face or at most a wry grimace.

These early novels are far more than just adventurous dives into the deep canyons of fantasy. They are more like mountain climbs to the edge of space. They can be disturbing, and intentionally so. Wells knew early on that his audiences enjoyed a good scare; and he enjoyed, in those prewar years of growing tension, placing human folly in cosmic perspective.

In writing *The Time Machine,* Wells claimed to draw his inspiration from Nathaniel Hawthorne, but there is also a touch of Poe in early drafts. Wells was fond of Voltaire, the French philosopher and satirist; he

respected but found little useful comparison with Jules
Verne, whose own satiric elements are often over-
looked. Most often, Wells likened himself to Jonathan
Swift, the sardonic Irish author of *Gulliver's Travels*.

The Time Machine was compared favorably in one
review to Robert Louis Stevenson's *Dr. Jekyll and Mr.
Hyde,* a masterpiece of psychological horror. *The Time
Machine*'s horrors are less moral than neutral, however. Its plan is not so much darkly psychological as
biological and *physical*. Whatever our psychology, our
class, our politics, Wells says, the laws of nature will
betray us. In the greater scheme of things, our personal lives and wishes seem to mean very little.

This sensation of doom and claustrophobia at the
end of life on Earth, and the end of Earth itself,
evokes a new kind of fear, a *cosmic* fear. In later
decades, writers as diverse as William Hope Hodgson,
H. P. Lovecraft, and Olaf Stapledon would expand
upon Wells's concepts and time scales, with extraordinary results upon philosophy and popular culture. The
universe would never look the same to us.

Years later, in 1934, Wells would write that horror
is easier to create than hope, or uplifting suggestions
for improving the human race. His science fiction novels, however, demand reactions entirely other than
paralyzed fear; they provide a clear-eyed perspective
of our place in the universe, a realistic sense of human
smallness, refreshing to this day in our world of simian
self-regard.

We still need the Wellsian anodyne of these brisk,
abrupt, and heated early novels, and in particular, we
still need *The Time Machine*.

How did a draper's assistant, son of a man variously
described as a cricketer, a gardener, and a shopkeeper,

with a sporadic education and in frequent ill health, come to put together something so rich, diverse, and utterly *new*?

H. G. Wells began by studying hard. He took advantage of an experiment in free schooling at the Normal School of Science (after 1890 renamed the Royal College of Science) to listen to some of the great voices and minds of his day. He read everything he could get his hands on: biology, geology, astronomy, and of course geometry. Victorians were masters at playing with geometric concepts, witness Lewis Carroll's *Alice* stories and Edwin A. Abbott's masterwork, *Flatland* (1884). (Abbott was not a mathematician, but a schoolmaster, as was Wells for a time.)

A fellow student, E. A. Hamilton-Gordon, presented a paper on the fourth dimension at a meeting of the Debating Society that bore a distinct (though perhaps coincidental) resemblance to an essay by C. H. Hinton called "What Is the Fourth Dimension?", published in 1884–1885 in his two-volume collection, *Scientific Romances*. Hamilton-Gordon's talk and possibly Hinton's essay are likely the prime influences on Wells's discussion of the fourth dimension and time travel.

Earlier still, topologist August Ferdinand Möbius (1790–1868) had described, among other wonders, the one-sided piece of paper that bears his name. Giving a longish strip of paper a half twist and then fastening the ends together produces a marvelous "vanishing" of one side. (Try it—ignore the glued or taped part, and run your finger around the entire surface . . . an endless loop! If one can *lose* geometric features, isn't it possible to *gain* a few, as well? An extra dimension, perhaps?)

Charles Darwin, Alfred Russel Wallace, T. H. Huxley, and other controversial biological thinkers had shown the scientific world that humans had evolved over deep time, and this implied that they could still evolve—in Huxley's opinion, not necessarily for the better, but almost certainly in adaptation to a dying world. Wells autographed a copy of the British edition of *The Time Machine* for Huxley in May 1895:

> *Dear Sir,*
> *I am sending you a little book that I fancy may be of interest to you. The central idea— that of degeneration following security—was the outcome of a certain amount of biological study. I daresay your position subjects you to a good many such displays of the range of authors but I have this much excuse—I was one of your pupils at the Royal College of Science and finally: the book is a very little one.*

Huxley died in June of that year. He probably never had time to read his student's novel.

The year 802,701, the last date specified in *The Time Machine,* was far more remote to a scientist in Wells's era than it might seem now. (Though very little science fiction even today ventures so far into the future.) The best scientific speculation of the time placed the age of the solar system at no more than fifteen to twenty-four million years, based on the probability that the sun was a combusting ball of gas.

This relatively brief span caused Darwinians and many geologists concern. The Darwinians needed great gulfs of time—certainly more than just tens of millions of years—to explain the diversity of life on Earth through slow and gradual evolution. The geologists saw evidence of processes occurring over hundreds of millions of years, possibly even billions of years.

Fusion of hydrogen into helium and heavier elements was of course unknown at the time. It wasn't until the 1920s and the researches of deep-sky astronomers like Edwin Hubble that the true size and age of the universe began to be understood, and the Darwinians and geologists could breathe easier. However, Wells's estimate of the time and nature of the death of the Earth was in agreement with the science of the time, and his description of the sun blossoming into a red giant is still accurate enough—though the Earth is likely to be swallowed by this future monstrosity and crisped, not frozen.

Wells acquired skepticism early in his life. As he wrote *The Time Machine,* he was unsure of what lay ahead for himself, much less the human race. Both personally and historically, the last decade of the nineteenth century was a time of danger and change. Engaged in an affair with future wife Amy Catherine Robbins (whom Wells would nickname "Jane"), recently separated from his first wife, cousin Isabel, and barely earning any kind of living, Wells likely began each day by being at least a little frightened.

Like T. H. Huxley, whose own upbringing was far from upper-crust, Wells distrusted the soothing religious and political babble of the day. Not for him the easy pathway to a gentleman's success and leisure. He could not trust the class system that would have relegated him, by birth alone, to obscurity; the son of a tradesman, Wells clearly saw that unearned privilege and inbred claims of intellectual supremacy draped England and Europe in a shroud of ill omen.

Consequently, his first work of fiction is dark, almost hopeless—but for the tiny hand of love offered by a future childlike member of the "upper" classes, Weena.

Later, Wells would regret this self-styled hat flipping and reliance on visceral emotions, aiming instead for a program of intellectual and moral reform, of disci-

plined hope and warnings of the bleaker prospects of
the twentieth century. Still, to his irritation, his early
scientific romances remained his most popular works.
He had done more than strike a chord; he had composed a new kind of symphony.

To the masses of readers around the world, especially in information-hungry America and England,
Wells became the prophet of science and a hopeful if
stern critic of political and technological progress.
Along the way, however, his reputation and his own
sense of self-worth were almost derailed by the very
violence he predicted with such prescience.

As Wells had feared, the ruling upper classes *did*
goof, and horribly, in both politics and military strategy. World War I killed ten million people and rav-
aged Europe. (Spanish influenza, possibly spread by
troop mobilizations and international trauma and
stress, killed tens of millions more.) Airplanes and di-
rigibles dropping bombs on civilian populations, so-
called "Land Ironclads" (tanks), and poison gas—all
predicted by Wells and all dire products of the science
that had fascinated Wells's audience before 1914—
were used and abused by incompetent, vicious, and
even demented politicians and generals.

As the bodies stacked up in uncounted piles—much
of a generation wasted—for many, the promise of science became indelibly tainted. The promise of the prewar modernists, an extraordinary blossom of art and
literature, was squashed. Hope and innovation turned
into a sense of intellectual and moral defeat, and the
drug that best dulled the pain, for some, was a suffo-
cating and hopeless irony.

An intellectual upper class had been forming for
decades that eschewed everything scientific and technological and adhered to a utopian mix of socialism

and elitist aesthetic principles. Before the war, artists
and thinkers like William Morris (1834–1896) and William Blake (1757–1827) had voiced strong criticisms
of rampant industrialization and untrammeled growth.
(Both retained an interest in spirituality and imaginative literature, however—Morris having produced fantasies that would later inspire Tolkien and others.)

The trauma of the war and subsequent social up-
heaval forced many writers and artists to align their
axes of culture with Marx and Freud, rejecting the so-
called pure sciences, as well as spirituality, and simul-
taneously shutting the door on fairy tales, ghost stories, myth, and almost all imaginative storytelling.

These new literary Brahmins may have blamed
Wells for the truth of the very warnings he had so
passionately shouted. Or more simply, they were tired
of his raucous and argumentative personality and his
extraordinary success. An unfortunate row between
former friends and correspondents, Wells and Henry
James (who died in 1916), widened the breach.

Once a valued member of the literary club, during
the war Wells began to be regarded as a self-
parodying buffoon, an outcast—and an anti-Jamesian.
His chief sin was that he was popular; but he also
understood the social implications of science better
than any man of his time, and still trumpeted rational
thought and the possibility of progress. His fiction was
intended for more than just aesthetic effect, and this,
for the Jamesians and others, became tiresome.

The man who had done so much to forecast the
twentieth century was regarded by an influential mi-
nority as shrill and inflexible, too smart for his own
good, and certainly not to be trusted. In literature,
some of the old prewar class system lived on through
the 1920s and 1930s, reduced to a parade of style,
fashion and irony, a Jamesian ghost haunting a twilight

world of pale upper-class emotions. Perversely, Wells still desired the approval of these old friends, yet at the same time mercilessly parodied them. Many could not find it in their hearts to put up with him.

Virginia Woolf announced, characteristically, that Wells was "passé."

Cast out of this new definition of literature, along with Wells, were science itself and, incidentally, that branch of the literature of ideas that was coming to be known as science fiction. Both have been ignored for decades in textbooks and history books, scrupulously replaced by the literature of manners, and by a strange variety of "social realism" intent on depicting a decaying world without science or scientists.

C. P. Snow's Two Cultures—science and the humanities—had split apart, to the detriment of both.

Buttressed in their ivory towers, after the atom bomb and the beginning of the space age, and certainly after the first moon landing, those who denied science began to look more and more like Wells's ineffectual Eloi. And sure enough, as Wells had predicted as early as 1893,[1] the literature of the masses, including science fiction, began to mock them, and then to absorb them—in short, to have them for lunch.

Much of academic literature and art went on life

[1] "The old literature was aristocratic, and this age is only the dawn of democracy. The old literature is full of subtle meanings, hinting quotations, faint allusions; it has a classical flavour, like the scent of lavender. The democracy will have none of your classics, it hates allusions and quotations; it likes a writer to be 'clear and sensible'. It is suspicious of being laughed at. . . . The old literature had a soft voice and a gentle insinuating manner; the new literature will be a thing of loud bawling books, shrieking headlines, and slovenly grammar." (Wells, unsigned, "The Literature of the Future: the Horoscope of Books," *The Pall Mall Gazette,* 11 October 1893.)

support, like a rare plant in a hothouse. Weedy and wild, impolite and scary, H. G. Wells lives on, inspiring millions. To this day, his works and the works of his intellectual children prosper in novels, stories, films, comic books, computer games, and all manner of new electronic media around the world.

Wells lived long enough to see another of his predictions—the atomic bomb—undergo a horrible birth in the skies over Japan. At the time of his death in 1946, this brilliant man, who had worked so hard for rationality and political planning, returned to his early days of pessimism, but with the harder, darker cast of despairing old age. Wells was convinced that the world was heading down the wrong path, possibly to utter nuclear destruction (*Mind at the End of Its Tether* [1946]).

Finally, he was wrong. Humanity survived the twentieth century. The gigantic and destructive tyrannies of the 1920s and 1930s are gone. The lingering Soviet empire is also gone (something he did foresee). The United States dominates world economics and politics, trading glances with a lumbering, renascent China, which would have made Wells—and most British writers—very uneasy.

The prospects are challenging. Dark days and light come and go in alteration, like the flickering of suns from the Time Traveller's perspective, but hope remains.

Weena's hand is still outstretched.

The Time Machine was Wells's first major publication, his first novel. It remains one of the most influential novels ever written, and easily one of the most exciting.

Time travel in fiction is common now, in hundreds

if not thousands of novels and stories, on television and in motion pictures. (Curiously, it may have been the early ancestors of motion pictures that provided the strongest metaphor for time travel—time as frames on a strip of film.) But before Wells, people had traveled in time only through mysterious forces (Mark Twain's brilliant *A Connecticut Yankee in King Arthur's Court*), suspended animation (Washington Irving's "Rip Van Winkle"), the aid of spirits (Dickens's "A Christmas Carol"), or the agencies of the gods.

Wells hinted that time travel might actually be scientifically feasible. *Using a machine, a feat of brilliant personal engineering, you or I,* he said, with barely a wink, *can travel into the future, or the past, at will.*

And to this day, there are reputable scientists (well, theoretical physicists) who believe that he may be right. Sometimes, they do not even wink.

Could one of us, someday, discover an unknown quantum principle, a trick of crystalline interplay between matter, space, and time, and create a machine that shivers at our touch like a leaf in the wind, caught between an infinity of split seconds and long, dim eons?

Is time travel possible? Or mere fantasy?

The answer depends on how young you are. As always, the past is for the old, and the future is for the young. Look around you.

As Ray Bradbury—another child of Wells—has pointed out, there are time machines everywhere.

—Greg Bear

THE
TIME MACHINE

1

THE TIME TRAVELLER (for so it will be convenient to speak of him) was expounding a recondite matter to us. His grey eyes shone and twinkled, and his usually pale face was flushed and animated. The fire burned brightly, and the soft radiance of the incandescent lights in the lilies of silver caught the bubbles that flashed and passed in our glasses. Our chairs, being his patents, embraced and caressed us rather than submitted to be sat upon, and there was that luxurious after-dinner atmosphere when thought runs gracefully free of the trammels of precision. And he put it to us in this way—marking the points with a lean forefinger—as we sat and lazily admired his earnestness over this new paradox (as we thought it:) and his fecundity.

"You must follow me carefully. I shall have to controvert one or two ideas that are almost universally accepted. The geometry, for instance, they taught you at school is founded on a misconception."

"Is not that rather a large thing to expect us to begin upon?" said Filby, an argumentative person with red hair.

"I do not mean to ask you to accept anything without reasonable ground for it. You will soon admit as much as I need from you. You know of course that a mathematical line, a line of thickness *nil*, has no real existence. They taught you that? Neither has a mathematical plane. These things are mere abstractions."

"That is all right," said the Psychologist.

"Nor, having only length, breadth, and thickness, can a cube have a real existence."

"There I object," said Filby. "Of course a solid body may exist. All real things————"

"So most people think. But wait a moment. Can an *instantaneous* cube exist?"

"Don't follow you," said Filby.

"Can a cube that does not last for any time at all, have a real existence?"

Filby became pensive. "Clearly," the Time Traveller proceeded, "any real body must have extension in *four* directions: it must have Length, Breadth, Thickness, and—Duration. But through a natural infirmity of the flesh, which I will explain to you in a moment, we incline to overlook this fact. There are really four dimensions, three which we call the three planes of Space, and a fourth, Time. There is, however, a tendency to draw an unreal distinction between the former three dimensions and the latter, because it happens that our consciousness moves intermittently in one direction along the latter from the beginning to the end of our lives."

"That," said a very young man, making spasmodic efforts to relight his cigar over the lamp; "that . . . very clear indeed."

"Now, it is very remarkable that this is so extensively overlooked," continued the Time Traveller, with a slight accession of cheerfulness. "Really this is what is meant by the Fourth Dimension, though some people who talk about the Fourth Dimension do not know they mean it. It is only another way of looking at Time. *There is no difference between Time and any of the three dimensions of Space except that our con-*

sciousness moves along it. But some foolish people have got hold of the wrong side of that idea. You have all heard what they have to say about this Fourth Dimension?"

"*I* have not," said the Provincial Mayor.

"It is simply this. That Space, as our mathematicians have it, is spoken of as having three dimensions, which one may call Length, Breadth, and Thickness, and is always definable by reference to three planes, each at right angles to the others. But some philosophical people have been asking why *three* dimensions particularly—why not another direction at right angles to the other three?—and have even tried to construct a Four-Dimension geometry. Professor Simon Newcomb was expounding this to the New York Mathematical Society only a month or so ago. You know how on a flat surface, which has only two dimensions, we can represent a figure of a three-dimensional solid, and similarly they think that by models of three dimensions they could represent one of four—if they could master the perspective of the thing. See?"

"I think so," murmured the Provincial Mayor; and, knitting his brows, he lapsed into an introspective state, his lips moving as one who repeats mystic words. "Yes, I think I see it now," he said after some time, brightening in a quite transitory manner.

"Well, I do not mind telling you I have been at work upon this geometry of Four Dimensions for some time. Some of my results are curious. For instance, here is a portrait of a man at eight years old, another at fifteen, another at seventeen, another at twenty-three, and so on. All these are evidently sections, as it were, Three-Dimensional representations of his Four-Dimensioned being, which is a fixed and unalterable thing.

"Scientific people," proceeded the Time Traveller,

after the pause required for the proper assimilation of this, "know very well that Time is only a kind of Space. Here is a popular scientific diagram, a weather record. This line I trace with my finger shows the movement of the barometer. Yesterday it was so high, yesterday night it fell, then this morning it rose again, and so gently upward to here. Surely the mercury did not trace this line in any of the dimensions of Space generally recognized? But certainly it traced such a line, and that line, therefore, we must conclude was along the Time-Dimension."

"But," said the Medical Man, staring hard at a coal in the fire, "if Time is really only a fourth dimension of Space, why is it, and why has it always been, regarded as something different? And why cannot we move in Time as we move about in the other dimensions of Space?"

The Time Traveller smiled. "Are you sure we can move freely in Space? Right and left we can go, backward and forward freely enough, and men always have done so. I admit we move freely in two dimensions. But how about up and down? Gravitation limits us there."

"Not exactly," said the Medical Man. "There are balloons."

"But before the balloons, save for spasmodic jumping and the inequalities of the surface, man had no freedom of vertical movement."

"Still they could move a little up and down," said the Medical Man.

"Easier, far easier down than up."

"And you cannot move at all in Time, you cannot get away from the present moment."

"My dear sir, that is just where you are wrong. That is just where the whole world has gone wrong. We are always getting away from the present moment. Our mental existences, which are immaterial and have no dimensions, are passing along the Time-Dimension with a uniform velocity from the cradle to the grave. Just as we should travel *down* if we began our existence fifty miles above the earth's surface."

"But the great difficulty is this," interrupted the Psychologist. "You *can* move about in all directions of Space, but you cannot move about in Time."

"That is the germ of my great discovery. But you are wrong to say that we cannot move about in Time. For instance, if I am recalling an incident very vividly I go back to the instant of its occurrence: I become absent-minded, as you say. I jump back for a moment. Of course we have no means of staying back for any length of Time, any more than a savage or an animal has of staying six feet above the ground. But a civilized man is better off than the savage in this respect. He can go up against gravitation in a balloon, and why should he not hope that ultimately he may be able to stop or accelerate his drift along the Time-Dimension, or even turn about and travel the other way?"

"Oh, *this*," began Filby, "is all————"

"Why not?" said the Time Traveller.

"It's against reason," said Filby.

"What reason?" said the Time Traveller.

"You can show black is white by argument," said Filby, "but you will never convince me."

"Possibly not," said the Time Traveller. "But now you begin to see the object of my investigations into the geometry of Four Dimensions. Long ago I had a vague inkling of a machine————"

"To travel through Time!" exclaimed the Very Young Man.

"That shall travel indifferently in any direction of Space and Time as the driver determines."

Filby contented himself with laughter.

"But I have experimental verification," said the Time Traveller.

"It would be remarkably convenient for the historian," the Psychologist suggested. "One might travel back and verify the accepted account of the Battle of Hastings, for instance!"

"Don't you think you would attract attention?" said the Medical Man. "Our ancestors had no great tolerance for anachronisms."

"One might get one's Greek from the very lips of Homer and Plato," the Very Young Man thought.

"In which case they would certainly plough you for the Little-go. The German Scholars have improved Greek so much."

"Then there is the future," said the Very Young Man. "Just think! One might invest all one's money, leave it to accumulate at interest, and hurry on ahead!" *thinking of personal gain*

"To discover a society," said I, "erected on a strictly communistic basis."

"Of all the wild extravagant theories!" began the Psychologist.

"Yes, so it seemed to me, and so I never talked of it until———"

"Experimental verification!" cried I. "You are going to verify *that?*"

"The experiment!" cried Filby, who was getting brain-weary.

"Let's see your experiment anyhow," said the Psychologist, "though it's all humbug, you know."

The Time Traveller smiled round at us. Then, still smiling faintly, and with his hands deep in his trousers pockets, he walked slowly out of the room, and we heard his slippers shuffling down the long passage to his laboratory.

The Psychologist looked at us. "I wonder what he's got?"

"Some sleight-of-hand trick or other," said the Medical Man, and Filby tried to tell us about a conjurer he had seen at Burslem; but before he had finished his preface the Time Traveller came back, and Filby's anecdote collapsed.

The thing the Time Traveller held in his hand was a glittering metallic framework, scarcely larger than a small clock, and very delicately made. There was ivory in it, and some transparent crystalline substance. And now I must be explicit, for this that follows—unless his explanation is to be accepted—is an absolutely unaccountable thing. He took one of the small octagonal tables that were scattered about the room, and set it in front of the fire, with two legs on the hearthrug. On this table he placed the mechanism. Then he drew up a chair, and sat down. The only other object on the table was a small shaded lamp, the bright light of which fell upon the model. There were also perhaps a dozen candles about, two in brass candlesticks upon the mantel and several in sconces, so that the room was brilliantly illuminated. I sat in a low arm-chair nearest the fire, and I drew this forward so as to be almost between the Time Traveller and the fire-place. Filby sat behind him, looking over his shoulder. The Medical Man and the Provincial Mayor watched him in profile from the right, the Psychologist from the left. The Very Young Man stood behind the Psychologist. We were all on the alert. It appears incredible to me that any kind of trick, however subtly conceived and however adroitly done, could have been played upon us under these conditions.

The Time Traveller looked at us, and then at the mechanism. "Well?" said the Psychologist.

"This little affair," said the Time Traveller, resting

his elbows upon the table and pressing his hands together above the apparatus, "is only a model. It is my plan for a machine to travel through time. You will notice that it looks singularly askew, and that there is an odd twinkling appearance about this bar, as though it was in some way unreal." He pointed to the part with his finger. "Also, here is one little white lever, and here is another."

The Medical Man got up out of his chair and peered into the thing. "It's beautifully made," he said.

"It took two years to make," retorted the Time Traveller. Then, when we had all imitated the action of the Medical Man, he said: "Now I want you clearly to understand that this lever, being pressed over, sends the machine gliding into the future, and this other reverses the motion. This saddle represents the seat of a time traveller. Presently I am going to press the lever, and off the machine will go. It will vanish, pass into future Time, and disappear. Have a good look at the thing. Look at the table too, and satisfy yourselves there is no trickery. I don't want to waste this model, and then be told I'm a quack."

There was a minute's pause perhaps. The Psychologist seemed about to speak to me, but changed his mind. Then the Time Traveller put forth his finger toward the lever. "No," he said suddenly. "Lend me your hand." And turning to the Psychologist, he took that individual's hand in his own and told him to put out his forefinger. So that it was the Psychologist himself who sent forth the model Time Machine on its interminable voyage. We all saw the lever turn. I am absolutely certain there was no trickery. There was a breath of wind, and the lamp flame jumped. One of the candles on the mantel was blown out, and the little machine suddenly swung round, became indistinct, was seen as a ghost for a second perhaps, as an eddy of faintly glittering brass and ivory; and it was gone—vanished! Save for the lamp the table was bare.

Everyone was silent for a minute. Then Filby said he was damned.

The Psychologist recovered from his stupor, and suddenly looked under the table. At that the Time Traveller laughed cheerfully. "Well?" he said, with a reminiscence of the Psychologist. Then, getting up, he went to the tobacco jar on the mantel, and with his back to us began to fill his pipe.

We stared at each other. "Look here," said the Medical Man, "are you in earnest about this? Do you seriously believe that that machine has travelled into time?"

"Certainly," said the Time Traveller, stooping to light a spill at the fire. Then he turned, lighting his pipe, to look at the Psychologist's face. (The Psychologist, to show that he was not unhinged, helped himself to a cigar and tried to light it uncut.) "What is more, I have a big machine nearly finished in there"—he indicated the laboratory—"and when that is put together I mean to have a journey on my own account."

"You mean to say that that machine has travelled into the future?" said Filby.

"Into the future or the past—I don't, for certain, know which."

After an interval the Psychologist had an inspiration. "It must have gone into the past if it has gone anywhere," he said.

"Why?" said the Time Traveller.

"Because I presume that it has not moved in space, and if it travelled into the future it would still be here all this time, since it must have travelled through this time."

"But," I said, "if it travelled into the past it would have been visible when we came first into this room;

and last Thursday when we were here; and the Thursday before that; and so forth!"

"Serious objections," remarked the Provincial Mayor, with an air of impartiality, turning towards the Time Traveller.

"Not a bit," said the Time Traveller, and, to the Psychologist: "You think. *You* can explain that. It's presentation below the threshold you know, diluted presentation."

"Of course," said the Psychologist, and reassured us. "That's a simple point of psychology. I should have thought of it. It's plain enough, and helps the paradox delightfully. We cannot see it, nor can we appreciate this machine, any more than we can the spoke of a wheel spinning, or a bullet flying through the air. If it is travelling through time fifty times or a hundred times faster than we are, if it gets through a minute while we get through a second, the impression it creates will of course be only one-fiftieth or one-hundredth of what it would make if it were not travelling in time. That's plain enough." He passed his hand through the space in which the machine had been. "You see?" he said, laughing.

We sat and stared at the vacant table for a minute or so. Then the Time Traveller asked us what we thought of it all.

"It sounds plausible enough to-night," said the Medical Man; "but wait until to-morrow. Wait for the common sense of the morning."

"Would you like to see the Time Machine itself?" asked the Time Traveller. And therewith, taking the lamp in his hand, he led the way down the long, draughty corridor to his laboratory. I remember vividly the flickering light, his queer, broad head in silhouette, the dance of the shadows, how we all followed him, puzzled but incredulous, and how there in the laboratory we beheld a larger edition of the little mechanism which we had seen vanish from before our eyes. Parts were of nickel, parts of ivory, parts had certainly been filed or sawn out of rock crystal. The thing was generally complete, but the twisted crystalline bars lay unfinished upon the bench beside some sheets of drawings, and I took one up for a better look at it. Quartz it seemed to be.

"Look here," said the Medical Man, "are you perfectly serious? Or is this a trick—like that ghost you showed us last Christmas?"

"Upon that machine," said the Time Traveller, holding the lamp aloft, "I intend to explore time. Is that plain? I was never more serious in my life."

None of us quite knew how to take it.

I caught Filby's eye over the shoulder of the Medical Man, and he winked at me solemnly.

2

I THINK that at that time none of us quite believed in the Time Machine. The fact is, the Time Traveller was one of those men who are too clever to be believed: you never felt that you saw all round him; you always suspected some subtle reserve, some ingenuity in ambush, behind his lucid frankness. Had Filby shown the model and explained the matter in the Time Traveller's words, we should have shown *him* far less scepticism. For we should have perceived his motives; a pork butcher could understand Filby. But the Time Traveller had more than a touch of whim among his elements, and we distrusted him. Things that would have made the fame of a less clever man seemed tricks in his hands. It is a mistake to do things too easily. The serious people who took him seriously never felt quite sure of his deportment; they were somehow aware that trusting their reputations for judgment with him was like furnishing a nursery with egg-shell china. So I don't think any of us said very much about time travelling in the interval between that Thursday and the next, though its odd potentialities ran, no doubt, in most of our minds: its plausibility, that is, its practical incredibleness, the curious possibilities of anachronism and of utter confusion it suggested. For my own part, I was particularly preoccupied with the trick of the model. That I remember discussing with the Medical Man, whom I met on Friday at the Linnaean. He said he had seen a similar thing at Tübingen, and laid considerable stress on the blowing out of the candle. But how the trick was done he could not explain.

The next Thursday I went again to Richmond—I suppose I was one of the Time Traveller's most constant guests—and, arriving late, found four or five men already assembled in his drawing-room. The Medical Man was standing before the fire with a sheet of paper in one hand and his watch in the other. I looked round for the Time Traveller, and—"It's half-past seven now," said the Medical Man. "I suppose we'd better have dinner?"

"Where's———?" said I, naming our host.

"You've just come? It's rather odd. He's unavoidably detained. He asks me in this note to lead off with dinner at seven if he's not back. Says he'll explain when he comes."

"It seems a pity to let the dinner spoil," said the Editor of a well-known daily paper; and thereupon the Doctor rang the bell.

The Psychologist was the only person besides the Doctor and myself who had attended the previous dinner. The other men were Blank, the Editor aforementioned, a certain journalist, and another—a quiet, shy man with a beard—whom I didn't know, and who, as far as my observation went, never opened his mouth all the evening. There was some speculation at the dinner-table about the Time Traveller's absence, and I suggested time travelling, in a half-jocular spirit. The Editor wanted that explained to him, and the Psychologist volunteered a wooden account of the "ingenious paradox and trick" we had witnessed that day week. He was in the midst of his exposition when the door

from the corridor opened slowly and without noise. I
was facing the door, and saw it first. "Hallo!" I said.
"At last!" And the door opened wider, and the Time
Traveller stood before us. I gave a cry of surprise.
"Good heavens! man, what's the matter?" cried the
Medical Man, who saw him next. And the whole table-
ful turned towards the door.

He was in an amazing plight. His coat was dusty
and dirty, and smeared with green down the sleeves;
his hair disordered, and as it seemed to me greyer—
either with dust and dirt or because its colour had
actually faded. His face was ghastly pale; his chin had
a brown cut on it—a cut half healed; his expression
was haggard and drawn, as by intense suffering. For
a moment he hesitated in the doorway, as if he had
been dazzled by the light. Then he came into the
room. He walked with just such a limp as I have seen
in footsore tramps. We stared at him in silence, expecting him to speak.

He said not a word, but came painfully to the table,
and made a motion towards the wine. The Editor filled
a glass of champagne, and pushed it towards him. He
drained it, and it seemed to do him good: for he
looked round the table, and the ghost of his old smile
flickered across his face. "What on earth have you
been up to, man?" said the Doctor. The Time Traveller did not seem to hear. "Don't let me disturb you,"
he said, with a certain faltering articulation. "I'm all
right." He stopped, held out his glass for more, and
took it off at a draught. "That's good," he said. His
eyes grew brighter, and a faint colour came into his
cheeks. His glance flickered over our faces with a certain dull approval, and then went round the warm and
comfortable room. Then he spoke again, still as if he
were feeling his way among his words. "I'm going to
wash and dress, and then I'll come down and explain

things. . . . Save me some of that mutton. I'm starving for a bit of meat."

He looked across at the Editor, who was a rare visitor, and hoped he was all right. The Editor began a question. "Tell you presently," said the Time Traveller. "I'm—funny. Be all right in a minute."

He put down his glass, and walked towards the staircase door. Again I remarked his lameness and the soft padding sound of his footfall, and standing up in my place, I saw his feet as he went out. He had nothing on them but a pair of tattered, blood-stained socks. Then the door closed upon him. I had half a mind to follow, till I remembered how he detested any fuss about himself. For a minute, perhaps, my mind was wool-gathering. Then, "Remarkable Behaviour of an Eminent Scientist," I heard the Editor say, thinking (after his wont) in headlines. And this brought my attention back to the bright dinner-table.

"What's the game?" said the Journalist. "Has he been doing the Amateur Cadger? I don't follow." I met the eye of the Psychologist, and read my own interpretation in his face. I thought of the Time Traveller limping painfully upstairs. I don't think any one else had noticed his lameness.

The first to recover completely from this surprise was the Medical Man, who rang the bell—the Time Traveller hated to have servants waiting at dinner—for a hot plate. At that the Editor turned to his knife and fork with a grunt, and the Silent Man followed suit. The dinner was resumed. Conversation was exclamatory for a little while, with gaps of wonderment; and then the Editor got fervent in his curiosity. "Does our friend eke out his modest income with a crossing? or has he his Nebuchadnezzar phases?" he inquired. "I feel assured it's this business of the Time Machine," I said, and took up the Psychologist's account of our previous meeting. The new guests were frankly incredulous. The Editor raised objections. "What *was* this time travelling? A man couldn't cover himself with dust by rolling in a paradox, could he?" And then, as the idea came home to him, he resorted to a caricature. Hadn't they any clothes-brushes in the Future? The Journalist, too, would not believe at any price, and joined the Editor in the easy work of heaping ridicule on the whole thing. They were both the new kind of journalist—very joyous, irreverent young men. "Our Special Correspondent in the Day after To-morrow reports," the Journalist was saying—or rather shouting—when the Time Traveller came back. He was dressed in ordinary evening clothes, and nothing save his haggard look remained of the change that had startled me.

"I say," said the Editor hilariously, "these chaps here say you have been travelling into the middle of next week! Tell us all about little Rosebery, will you? What will you take for the lot?"

The Time Traveller came to the place reserved for him without a word. He smiled quietly, in his old way. "Where's my mutton?" he said. "What a treat it is to stick a fork into meat again!"

"Story!" cried the Editor.

"Story be damned!" said the Time Traveller. "I want something to eat. I won't say a word until I get some peptone into my arteries. Thanks. And the salt."

"One word," said I. "Have you been time travelling?"

"Yes," said the Time Traveller, with his mouth full, nodding his head.

"I'd give a shilling a line for a verbatim note," said the Editor. The Time Traveller pushed his glass towards the Silent Man and rang it with his fingernail; at which the Silent Man, who had been staring at his face, started convulsively, and poured him wine. The rest of the dinner was uncomfortable. For my own part, sudden questions kept on rising to my lips, and I dare say it was the same with the others. The Journalist tried to relieve the tension by telling anecdotes of Hettie Potter. The Time Traveller devoted his attention to his dinner, and displayed the appetite of a tramp. The Medical Man smoked a cigarette, and watched the Time Traveller through his eyelashes. The Silent Man seemed even more clumsy than usual, and drank champagne with regularity and determination out of sheer nervousness. At last the Time Traveller pushed his plate away, and looked round us. "I suppose I must apologize," he said. "I was simply starving. I've had a most amazing time." He reached out his hand for a cigar, and cut the end. "But come into the smoking-room. It's too long a story to tell over greasy plates." And ringing the bell in passing, he led the way into the adjoining room.

"You have told Blank, and Dash, and Chose about the machine?" he said to me, leaning back in his easy-chair and naming the three new guests.

"But the thing's a mere paradox," said the Editor.

"I can't argue to-night. I don't mind telling you the story, but I can't argue. I will," he went on, "tell you the story of what has happened to me, if you like, but you must refrain from interruptions. I want to tell it. Badly. Most of it will sound like lying. So be it! It's true—every word of it, all the same. I was in my laboratory at four o'clock, and since then . . . I've lived eight days . . . such days as no human being ever lived before! I'm nearly worn out, but I shan't sleep till I've told this thing over to you. Then I shall go to bed. But no interruptions! Is it agreed?"

"Agreed," said the Editor, and the rest of us echoed "Agreed." And with that the Time Traveller began his story as I have set it forth. He sat back in his chair at first, and spoke like a weary man. Afterwards he got more animated. In writing it down I feel with only too much keenness the inadequacy of pen and ink—and, above all, my own inadequacy—to express its quality. You read, I will suppose, attentively enough; but you cannot see the speaker's white, sincere face in the bright circle of the little lamp, nor hear the intonation of his voice. You cannot know how his expression followed the turns of his story! Most of us hearers were in shadow, for the candles in the smoking-room had not been lighted, and only the face of the Journalist and the legs of the Silent Man from the knees downward were illuminated. At first we glanced now and again at each other. After a time we ceased to do that, and looked only at the Time Traveller's face.

3

"I TOLD some of you last Thursday of the principles of the Time Machine, and showed you the actual thing itself, incomplete in the workshop. There it is now, a little travel-worn, truly; and one of the ivory bars is cracked, and a brass rail bent; but the rest of it's sound enough. I expected to finish it on Friday, but on Friday, when the putting together was nearly done, I found that one of the nickel bars was exactly one inch too short, and this I had to get remade; so that the thing was not complete until this morning. It was at ten o'clock to-day that the first of all Time Machines began its career. I gave it a last tap, tried all the screws again, put one more drop of oil on the quartz rod, and sat myself in the saddle. I suppose a suicide who holds a pistol to his skull feels much the same wonder at what will come next as I felt then. I took the starting lever in one hand and the stopping one in the other, pressed the first, and almost immediately the second. I seemed to reel; I felt a nightmare sensation of falling; and looking round, I saw the laboratory exactly as before. Had anything happened? For a moment I suspected that my intellect had tricked me. Then I noted the clock. A moment before, as it seemed, it had stood at a minute or so past ten; now it was nearly half-past three!

"I drew a breath, set my teeth, gripped the starting lever with both hands, and went off with a thud. The laboratory got hazy and went dark. Mrs. Watchett came in and walked, apparently without seeing me, towards the garden door. I suppose it took her a minute or so to traverse the place, but to me she seemed to shoot across the room like a rocket. I pressed the lever over to its extreme position. The night came like the turning out of a lamp, and in another moment came to-morrow. The laboratory grew faint and hazy, then fainter and ever fainter. To-morrow night came black, then day again, night again, day again, faster and faster still. An eddying murmur filled my ears, and a strange, dumb confusedness descended on my mind.

"I am afraid I cannot convey the peculiar sensations of time travelling. They are excessively unpleasant. There is a feeling exactly like that one has upon a switchback—of a helpless headlong motion! I felt the same horrible anticipation, too, of an imminent smash. As I put on pace, night followed day like the flapping of a black wing. The dim suggestion of the laboratory seemed presently to fall away from me, and I saw the sun hopping swiftly across the sky, leaping it every minute, and every minute marking a day. I supposed the laboratory had been destroyed and I had come into the open air. I had a dim impression of scaffolding, but I was already going too fast to be conscious of any moving things. The slowest snail that ever crawled dashed by too fast for me. The twinkling succession of darkness and light was excessively painful to the eye. Then, in the intermittent darknesses, I saw the moon spinning swiftly through her quarters from new to full, and had a faint glimpse of the circling stars. Presently, as I went on, still gaining velocity, the palpitation of night and day merged into one continuous greyness; the sky took on a wonderful deepness of blue, a splendid luminous color like that of early twilight; the jerking sun became a streak of fire, a brilliant arch, in space; the moon a fainter fluctuating band; and I could see nothing of the stars, save now and then a brighter circle flickering in the blue.

"The landscape was misty and vague. I was still on the hill-side upon which this house now stands, and the shoulder rose above me grey and dim. I saw trees growing and changing like puffs of vapour, now brown, now green; they grew, spread, shivered, and passed away. I saw huge buildings rise up faint and fair, and pass like dreams. The whole surface of the earth seemed changed—melting and flowing under my eyes. The little hands upon the dials that registered my speed raced round faster and faster. Presently I noted that the sun belt swayed up and down, from solstice to solstice, in a minute or less, and that consequently my pace was over a year a minute; and minute by minute the white snow flashed across the world, and vanished, and was followed by the bright, brief green of spring.

"The unpleasant sensations of the start were less poignant now. They merged at last into a kind of hysterical exhilaration. I remarked indeed a clumsy swaying of the machine, for which I was unable to account. But my mind was too confused to attend to it, so with a kind of madness growing upon me, I flung myself into futurity. At first I scarce thought of stopping, scarce thought of anything but these new sensations. But presently a fresh series of impressions grew up in my mind—a certain curiosity and therewith a certain dread—until at last they took complete possession of me. What strange developments of humanity, what wonderful advances upon our rudimentary civilization, I thought, might not appear when I came to look nearly into the dim elusive world that raced and fluctuated before my eyes! I saw great and splendid architecture rising about me, more massive than any buildings of our own time, and yet, as it seemed, built of glimmer and mist. I saw a richer green flow up the hill-side, and remain there without any wintry intermission. Even through the veil of my confusion the earth seemed very fair. And so my mind came round to the business of stopping.

"The peculiar risk lay in the possibility of my finding some substance in the space which I, or the machine, occupied. So long as I travelled at a high velocity through time, this scarcely mattered; I was, so to speak, attenuated—was slipping like a vapour through the interstices of intervening substances! But to come to a stop involved the jamming of myself, molecule by molecule, into whatever lay in my way; meant bringing my atoms into such intimate contact with those of the obstacle that a profound chemical reaction—possibly a far-reaching explosion—would result, and blow myself and my apparatus out of all possible dimensions—into the Unknown. This possibility had occurred to me again and again while I was making the machine; but then I had cheerfully accepted it as an unavoidable risk—one of the risks a man has got to take! Now the risk was inevitable, I no longer saw it in the same cheerful light. The fact is that, insensibly, the absolute strangeness of everything, the sickly jarring and swaying of the machine, above all, the feeling of prolonged falling, had absolutely upset my nerve. I told myself that I could never stop, and with a gust of petulance I resolved to stop forthwith. Like an impatient fool, I lugged over the lever, and incontinently the thing went reeling over, and I was flung headlong through the air.

"There was the sound of a clap of thunder in my

ears. I may have been stunned for a moment. A pitiless hail was hissing round me, and I was sitting on soft turf in front of the overset machine. Everything still seemed grey, but presently I remarked that the confusion in my ears was gone. I looked round me. I was on what seemed to be a little lawn in a garden, surrounded by rhododendron bushes, and I noticed that their mauve and purple blossoms were dropping in a shower under the beating of the hailstones. The rebounding, dancing hail hung in a cloud over the machine, and drove along the ground like smoke. In a moment I was wet to the skin. 'Fine hospitality,' said I, 'to a man who has travelled innumerable years to see you.'

"Presently I thought what a fool I was to get wet. I stood up and looked round me. A colossal figure, carved apparently in some white stone, loomed indistinctly beyond the rhododendrons through the hazy downpour. But all else of the world was invisible.

"My sensations would be hard to describe. As the columns of hail grew thinner, I saw the white figure more distinctly. It was very large, for a silver birch-tree touched its shoulder. It was of white marble, in shape something like a winged sphinx, but the wings, instead of being carried vertically at the sides, were spread so that it seemed to hover. The pedestal, it appeared to me, was of bronze, and was thick with verdigris. It chanced that the face was towards me; the sightless eyes seemed to watch me; there was the faint shadow of a smile on the lips. It was greatly weather-worn, and that imparted an unpleasant suggestion of disease. I stood looking at it for a little space—half a minute, perhaps, or half an hour. It seemed to advance and to recede as the hail drove before it denser or thinner. At last I tore my eyes from it for a moment, and saw that the hail curtain had worn threadbare, and that the sky was lightening with the promise of the sun.

"I looked up again at the crouching white shape, and the full temerity of my voyage came suddenly upon me. What might appear when that hazy curtain was altogether withdrawn? What might not have happened to men? What if cruelty had grown into a common passion? What if in this interval the race had lost its manliness, and had developed into something inhuman, unsympathetic, and overwhelmingly powerful? I might seem some old-world savage animal, only the more dreadful and disgusting for our common likeness—a foul creature to be incontinently slain.

"Already I saw other vast shapes—huge buildings with intricate parapets and tall columns, with a wooded hill-side dimly creeping in upon me through the lessening storm. I was seized with a panic fear. I turned frantically to the Time Machine, and strove hard to readjust it. As I did so the shafts of the sun smote through the thunderstorm. The grey downpour was swept aside and vanished like the trailing garments of a ghost. Above me, in the intense blue of the summer sky, some faint brown shreds of cloud whirled into nothingness. The great buildings about me stood out clear and distinct, shining with the wet of the thunderstorm, and picked out in white by the unmelted hailstones piled along their courses. I felt naked in a strange world. I felt as perhaps a bird may feel in the clear air, knowing the hawk wings above can and will swoop. My fear grew to frenzy. I took a breathing space, set my teeth, and again grappled fiercely, wrist and knee, with the machine. It gave under my desperate onset and turned over. It struck my chin violently. One hand on the saddle, the other on the lever, I stood panting heavily in attitude to mount again.

"But with this recovery of a prompt retreat my courage recovered. I looked more curiously and less fearfully at this world of the remote future. In a circular opening, high up in the wall of the nearer house, I saw a group of figures clad in rich soft robes. They had seen me, and their faces were directed towards me.

"Then I heard voices approaching me. Coming through the bushes by the White Sphinx were the heads and shoulders of men running. One of these emerged in a pathway leading straight to the little lawn upon which I stood with my machine. He was a slight creature—perhaps four feet high—clad in a purple tunic, girdled at the waist with a leather belt. Sandals or buskins—I could not clearly distinguish which—were on his feet; his legs were bare to the knees, and his head was bare. Noticing that, I noticed for the first time how warm the air was.

"He struck me as being a very beautiful and graceful creature, but indescribably frail. His flushed face reminded me of the more beautiful kind of consumptive—that hectic beauty of which we used to hear so much. At the sight of him I suddenly regained confidence. I took my hands from the machine.

4

"IN ANOTHER MOMENT we were standing face to face, I and this fragile thing out of futurity. He came straight up to me and laughed into my eyes. The absence from his bearing of any sign of fear struck me at once. Then he turned to the two others who were following him and spoke to them in a strange and very sweet and liquid tongue.

"There were others coming, and presently a little group of perhaps eight or ten of these exquisite creatures were about me. One of them addressed me. It came into my head, oddly enough, that my voice was too harsh and deep for them. So I shook my head, and pointing to my ears, shook it again. He came a step forward, hesitated, and then touched my hand. Then I felt other soft little tentacles upon my back and shoulders. They wanted to make sure I was real. There was nothing in this at all alarming. Indeed, there was something in these pretty little people that inspired confidence—a graceful gentleness, a certain childlike ease. And besides, they looked so frail that I could fancy myself flinging the whole dozen of them about like nine-pins. But I made a sudden motion to warn them when I saw their little pink hands feeling at the Time Machine. Happily then, when it was not too late, I thought of a danger I had hitherto forgot-

ten, and reaching over the bars of the machine I un-
screwed the little levers that would set it in motion,
and put these in my pocket. Then I turned again to
see what I could do in the way of communication.

"And then, looking more nearly into their features,
I saw some further peculiarities in their Dresden-china
type of prettiness. Their hair, which was uniformly
curly, came to a sharp end at the neck and cheek;
there was not the faintest suggestion of it on the face,
and their ears were singularly minute. The mouths
were small, with bright red, rather thin lips, and the
little chins ran to a point. The eyes were large and
mild; and—this may seem egotism on my part—I fancied even that there was a certain lack of the interest
I might have expected in them.

"As they made no effort to communicate with me,
but simply stood round me smiling and speaking in
soft cooing notes to each other, I began the conversation. I pointed to the Time Machine and to myself.
Then hesitating for a moment how to express time, I
pointed to the sun. At once a quaintly pretty little
figure in chequered purple and white followed my gesture, and then astonished me by imitating the sound
of thunder.

"For a moment I was staggered, though the import
of his gesture was plain enough. The question had
come into my mind abruptly: were these creatures
fools? You may hardly understand how it took me.
You see I had always anticipated that the people of
the year Eight Hundred and Two Thousand odd
would be incredibly in front of us in knowledge, art,
everything. Then one of them suddenly asked me a
question that showed him to be on the intellectual
level of one of our five-year-old children—asked me,
in fact, if I had come from the sun in a thunderstorm!
It let loose the judgment I had suspended upon their

clothes, their frail light limbs, and fragile features. A flow of disappointment rushed across my mind. For a moment I felt that I had built the Time Machine in vain.

"I nodded, pointed to the sun, and gave them such a vivid rendering of a thunderclap as startled them. They all withdrew a pace or so and bowed. Then came one laughing towards me, carrying a chain of beautiful flowers altogether new to me, and put it about my neck. The idea was received with melodious applause; and presently they were all running to and fro for flowers, and laughingly flinging them upon me until I was almost smothered with blossom. You who have never seen the like can scarcely imagine what delicate and wonderful flowers countless years of culture had created. Then someone suggested that their plaything should be exhibited in the nearest building, and so I was led past the sphinx of white marble, which had seemed to watch me all the while with a smile at my astonishment, towards a vast grey edifice of fretted stone. As I went with them the memory of my confident anticipations of a profoundly grave and intellectual posterity came, with irresistible merriment, to my mind.

"The building had a huge entry, and was altogether of colossal dimensions. I was naturally most occupied with the growing crowd of little people, and with the big open portals that yawned before me shadowy and mysterious. My general impression of the world I saw over their heads was a tangled waste of beautiful bushes and flowers, a long-neglected and yet weedless garden. I saw a number of tall spikes of strange white flowers, measuring a foot perhaps across the spread of the waxen petals. They grew scattered, as if wild, among the variegated shrubs, but, as I say, I did not examine them closely at this time. The Time Machine was left deserted on the turf among the rhododendrons.

"The arch of the doorway was richly carved, but naturally I did not observe the carving very narrowly, though I fancied I saw suggestions of old Phoenician decorations as I passed through, and it struck me that they were very badly broken and weather-worn. Several more brightly clad people met me in the doorway, and so we entered, I, dressed in dingy nineteenth-century garments, looking grotesque enough, garlanded with flowers, and surrounded by an eddying mass of bright, soft-colored robes and shining white limbs, in a melodious whirl of laughter and laughing speech.

"The big doorway opened into a proportionately great hall hung with brown. The roof was in shadow, and the windows, partially glazed with coloured glass and partially unglazed, admitted a tempered light. The floor was made up of huge blocks of some very hard white metal, not plates nor slabs—blocks, and it was so much worn, as I judged by the going to and fro of past generations, as to be deeply channelled along the more frequented ways. Transverse to the length were innumerable tables made of slabs of polished stone, raised perhaps a foot from the floor, and upon these were heaps of fruits. Some I recognized as a kind of hypertrophied raspberry and orange, but for the most part they were strange.

"Between the tables were scattered a great number of cushions. Upon these my conductors seated themselves, signing for me to do likewise. With a pretty absence of ceremony they began to eat the fruit with their hands, flinging peel and stalks, and so forth, into the round openings in the sides of the tables. I was not loath to follow their example, for I felt thirsty and hungry. As I did so I surveyed the hall at my leisure.

"And perhaps the thing that struck me most was its dilapidated look. The stained-glass windows, which displayed only a geometrical pattern, were broken in many places, and the curtains that hung across the lower end were thick with dust. And it caught my eye that the corner of the marble table near me was fractured. Nevertheless, the general effect was extremely rich and picturesque. There were, perhaps, a couple of hundred people dining in the hall, and most of them, seated as near to me as they could come, were watching me with interest, their little eyes shining over the fruit they were eating. All were clad in the same soft, and yet strong, silky material.

"Fruit, by the by, was all their diet. These people of the remote future were strict vegetarians, and while I was with them, in spite of some carnal cravings, I had to be frugivorous also. Indeed, I found afterwards that horses, cattle, sheep, dogs, had followed the Ichthyosaurus into extinction. But the fruits were very delightful; one, in particular, that seemed to be in season all the time I was there—a floury thing in a three-sided husk—was especially good, and I made it my staple. At first I was puzzled by all these strange fruits, and by the strange flowers I saw, but later I began to perceive their import.

"However, I am telling you of my fruit dinner in the distant future now. So soon as my appetite was a little checked, I determined to make a resolute attempt to learn the speech of these new men of mine. Clearly that was the next thing to do. The fruits seemed a convenient thing to begin upon, and holding one of these up I began a series of interrogative sounds and gestures. I had some considerable difficulty in conveying my meaning. At first my efforts met with a stare of surprise or inextinguishable laughter, but presently a fair-haired little creature seemed to grasp my intention and repeated a name. They had to chatter and explain the business at great length to each other, and my first attempts to make the exquisite little sounds of their language caused an immense amount of amusement. However, I felt like a schoolmaster amidst children, and persisted, and presently I had a score of noun substantives at least at my command; and then I got to demonstrative pronouns, and even the verb 'to eat.' But it was slow work, and the little people soon tired and wanted to get away from my interrogations, so I determined, rather of necessity, to let them give their lessons in little doses when they felt inclined. And very little doses I found they were before long, for I never met people more indolent or more easily fatigued.

"A queer thing I soon discovered about my little hosts, and that was their lack of interest. They would come to me with eager cries of astonishment, like children, but like children they would soon stop examining me and wander away after some other toy. The dinner and my conversational beginnings ended, I noted for the first time that almost all those who had surrounded me at first were gone. It is odd, too, how speedily I came to disregard these little people. I went out through the portal into the sunlit world again so soon as my hunger was satisfied. I was continually meeting more of these men of the future, who would follow me a little distance, chatter and laugh about me, and, having smiled and gesticulated in a friendly way, leave me again to my own devices.

"The calm of evening was upon the world as I emerged from the great hall, and the scene was lit by the warm glow of the setting sun. At first things were very confusing. Everything was so entirely different from the world I had known—even the flowers. The big building I had left was situated on the slope of a

broad river valley, but the Thames had shifted perhaps
a mile from its present position. I resolved to mount
to the summit of a crest, perhaps a mile and a half
away, from which I could get a wider view of this our
planet in the year Eight Hundred and Two Thousand
Seven Hundred and One A.D. For that, I should explain, was the date the little dials of my machine
recorded.

"As I walked I was watchful for every impression
that could possibly help to explain the condition of
ruinous splendour in which I found the world—for
ruinous it was. A little way up the hill for instance,
was a great heap of granite, bound together by masses
of aluminium, a vast labyrinth of precipitous walls and
crumbled heaps, amidst which were thick heaps of
very beautiful pagoda-like plants—nettles possibly—
but wonderfully tinted with brown about the leaves,
and incapable of stinging. It was evidently the derelict
remains of some vast structure, to what end built I
could not determine. It was here that I was destined,
at a later date, to have a very strange experience—
the first intimation of a still stranger discovery—but
of that I will speak in its proper place.

"Looking round with a sudden thought, from a ter-
race on which I rested for a while, I realized that there
were no small houses to be seen. Apparently the single
house, and possibly even the household, had vanished.
Here and there among the greenery were palace-like
buildings, but the house and the cottage, which form
such characteristic features of our own English landscape, had disappeared.

" 'Communism,' said I to myself.

"And on the heels of that came another thought. I
looked at the half-dozen little figures that were following me. Then, in a flash, I perceived that all had the

same form of costume, the same soft hairless visage, and the same girlish rotundity of limb. It may seem strange, perhaps, that I had not noticed this before. But everything was so strange. Now, I saw the fact plainly enough. In costume, and in all the differences of texture and bearing that now mark off the sexes from each other, these people of the future were alike. And the children seemed to my eyes to be but the miniatures of their parents. I judged, then, that the children of that time were extremely precocious, physically at least, and I found afterwards abundant verification of my opinion.

"Seeing the ease and security in which these people were living, I felt that this close resemblance of the sexes was after all what one would expect; for the strength of a man and the softness of a woman, the institution of the family, and the differentiation of occupations are mere militant necessities of an age of physical force; where population is balanced and abundant, much child-bearing becomes an evil rather than a blessing to the State; where violence comes but rarely and offspring are secure, there is less necessity—indeed there is no necessity—for an efficient family, and the specialization of the sexes with reference to their children's needs disappears. We see some beginnings of this even in our own time, and in this future age it was complete. This, I must remind you, was my speculation at the time. Later, I was to appreciate how far it fell short of the reality.

"While I was musing upon these things, my attention was attracted by a pretty little structure, like a well under a cupola. I thought in a transitory way of the oddness of wells still existing, and then resumed the thread of my speculations. There were no large buildings towards the top of the hill, and as my walking powers were evidently miraculous, I was presently left alone for the first time. With a strange sense of freedom and adventure I pushed on up to the crest.

"There I found a seat of some yellow metal that I did not recognize, corroded in places with a kind of pinkish rust and half smothered in soft moss, the arm-rests cast and filed into the resemblance of griffins' heads. I sat down on it, and I surveyed the broad view of our old world under the sunset of that long day. It was as sweet and fair a view as I have ever seen. The sun had already gone below the horizon and the west was flaming gold, touched with some horizontal bars of purple and crimson. Below was the valley of the Thames, in which the river lay like a band of bur-nished steel. I have already spoken of the great pal-aces dotted about among the variegated greenery, some in ruins and some still occupied. Here and there rose a white or silvery figure in the waste garden of the earth, here and there came the sharp vertical line of some cupola or obelisk. There were no hedges, no signs of proprietary rights, no evidences of agriculture; the whole earth had become a garden.

"So watching, I began to put my interpretation upon the things I had seen, and as it shaped itself to me that evening, my interpretation was something in this way. (Afterwards I found I had got only a half-truth—or only a glimpse of one facet of the truth.)

"It seemed to me that I had happened upon human-ity upon the wane. The ruddy sunset set me thinking of the sunset of mankind. For the first time I began to realize an odd consequence of the social effort in which we are at present engaged. And yet, come to think, it is a logical consequence enough. Strength is the outcome of need; security sets a premium on fee-bleness. The work of ameliorating the conditions of life—the true civilizing process that makes life more and more secure—had gone steadily on to a climax. One triumph of a united humanity over Nature had followed another. Things that are now mere dreams had become projects deliberately put in hand and carried forward. And the harvest was what I saw!

"After all, the sanitation and the agriculture of today are still in the rudimentary stage. The science of our time has attacked but a little department of the field of human disease, but, even so, it spreads its operations very steadily and persistently. Our agriculture and horticulture destroy a weed just here and there and cultivate perhaps a score or so of wholesome plants, leaving the greater number to fight out a balance as they can. We improve our favourite plants and animals—and how few they are—gradually by selective breeding; now a new and better peach, now a seedless grape, now a sweeter and larger flower, now a more convenient breed of cattle. We improve them gradually, because our ideals are vague and tentative, and our knowledge is very limited; because Nature, too, is shy and slow in our clumsy hands. Some day all this will be better organized, and still better. That is the drift of the current in spite of the eddies. The whole world will be intelligent, educated, and cooperating; things will move faster and faster towards the subjugation of Nature. In the end, wisely and carefully we shall readjust the balance of animal and vegetable life to suit our human needs.

"This adjustment, I say, must have been done, and done well; done indeed for all Time, in the space of Time across which my machine had leaped. The air was free from gnats, the earth from weeds or fungi; everywhere were fruits and sweet and delightful flowers; brilliant butterflies flew hither and thither. The ideal of preventive medicine was attained. Diseases had been stamped out. I saw no evidence of any contagious diseases during all my stay. And I shall have to tell you later that even the processes of putrefaction and decay had been profoundly affected by these changes.

"Social triumphs, too, had been effected. I saw mankind housed in splendid shelters, gloriously clothed, and as yet I had found them engaged in no toil. There were no signs of struggle, neither social nor economical struggle. The shop, the advertisement, traffic, all that commerce which constitutes the body of our world, was gone. It was natural on that golden evening that I should jump at the idea of a social paradise. The difficulty of increasing population had been met, I guessed, and population had ceased to increase.

"But with this change in condition comes inevitably adaptations to the change. What, unless biological science is a mass of errors, is the cause of human intelligence and vigour? Hardship and freedom: conditions under which the active, strong, and subtle survive and the weaker go to the wall; conditions that put a premium upon the loyal alliance of capable men, upon self-restraint, patience, and decision. And the institution of the family, and the emotions that arise therein, the fierce jealousy, the tenderness for offspring, parental self-devotion, all found their justification and support in the imminent dangers of the young. *Now*, where are these imminent dangers? There is a sentiment arising, and it will grow, against connubial jealousy, against fierce maternity, against passion of all sorts; unnecessary things now, and things that make us uncomfortable, savage survivals, discords in a refined and pleasant life.

"I thought of the physical slightness of the people, their lack of intelligence, and those big abundant ruins, and it strengthened my belief in a perfect conquest of Nature. For after the battle comes Quiet. Humanity had been strong, energetic, and intelligent, and had used all its abundant vitality to alter the conditions under which it lived. And now came the reaction of the altered conditions.

"Under the new conditions of perfect comfort and security, that restless energy, that with us is strength, would become weakness. Even in our own time certain tendencies and desires, once necessary to survival, are a constant source of failure. Physical courage and the love of battle, for instance, are no great help—may even be hindrances—to a civilized man. And in a state of physical balance and security, power, intellectual as well as physical, would be out of place. For countless years I judged there had been no danger of war or solitary violence, no danger from wild beasts, no wasting disease to require strength of constitution, no need of toil. For such a life, what we should call the weak are as well equipped as the strong, are indeed no longer weak. Better equipped indeed they are, for the strong would be fretted by an energy for which there was no outlet. No doubt the exquisite beauty of the buildings I saw was the outcome of the last surgings of the now purposeless energy of mankind before it settled down into perfect harmony with the conditions under which it lived—the flourish of that triumph which began the last great peace. This has ever been the fate of energy in security; it takes to art and to eroticism, and then come languor and decay.

"Even this artistic impetus would at last die away—had almost died in the Time I saw. To adorn themselves with flowers, to dance, to sing in the sunlight: so much was left of the artistic spirit, and no more. Even that would fade in the end into a contented inactivity. We are kept keen on the grindstone of pain and necessity, and, it seemed to me, that here was that hateful grindstone broken at last!

"As I stood there in the gathering dark I thought that in this simple explanation I had mastered the problem of the world—mastered the whole secret of these delicious people. Possibly the checks they had devised for the increase of population had succeeded too well, and their numbers had rather diminished than kept stationary. That would account for the abandoned ruins. Very simple was my explanation, and plausible enough—as most wrong theories are!

5

"As I stood there musing over this too perfect triumph of man, the full moon, yellow and gibbous, came up out of an overflow of silver light in the north-east. The bright little figures ceased to move about below, a noiseless owl flitted by, and I shivered with the chill of the night. I determined to descend and find where I could sleep.

"I looked for the building I knew. Then my eye travelled along to the figure of the White Sphinx upon the pedestal of bronze, growing distinct as the light of the rising moon grew brighter. I could see the silver birch against it. There was the tangle of rhododendron bushes, black in the pale light, and there was the little lawn. I looked at the lawn again. A queer doubt chilled my complacency. 'No,' said I stoutly to myself, 'that was not the lawn.'

"But it *was* the lawn. For the white leprous face of the sphinx was towards it. Can you imagine what I felt as this conviction came home to me? But you cannot. The Time Machine was gone!

"At once, like a lash across the face, came the possibility of losing my own age, of being left helpless in this strange new world. The bare thought of it was an actual physical sensation. I could feel it grip me at the throat and stop my breathing. In another moment I was in a passion of fear and running with great leaping strides down the slope. Once I fell headlong and cut my face; I lost no time in stanching the blood, but jumped up and ran on, with a warm trickle down my cheek and chin. All the time I ran I was saying to myself: 'They have moved it a little, pushed it under the bushes out of the way.' Nevertheless, I ran with all my might. All the time, with the certainty that sometimes comes with excessive dread, I knew that such assurance was folly, knew instinctively that the machine was removed out of my reach. My breath came with pain. I suppose I covered the whole distance from the hill crest to the little lawn, two miles perhaps, in ten minutes. And I am not a young man. I cursed aloud, as I ran, at my confident folly in leaving the machine, wasting good breath thereby. I cried aloud, and none answered. Not a creature seemed to be stirring in that moonlit world.

"When I reached the lawn my worst fears were realized. Not a trace of the thing was to be seen. I felt faint and cold when I faced the empty space among the black tangle of bushes. I ran round it furiously, as if the thing might be hidden in a corner, and then stopped abruptly, with my hands clutching my hair. Above me towered the sphinx, upon the bronze pedestal, white, shining, leprous, in the light of the rising moon. It seemed to smile in mockery of my dismay.

"I might have consoled myself by imagining the little people had put the mechanism in some shelter for me, had I not felt assured of their physical and intellectual inadequacy. That is what dismayed me: the sense of some hitherto unsuspected power, through whose intervention my invention had vanished. Yet, for one thing I felt assured: unless some other age had produced its exact duplicate, the machine could not have moved in time. The attachment of the levers—I

will show you the method later—prevented anyone
from tampering with it in that way when they were
removed. It had moved, and was hid, only in space.
But then, where could it be?

"I think I must have had a kind of frenzy. I remember running violently in and out among the moonlit
bushes all round the sphinx, and startling some white
animal that, in the dim light, I took for a small deer.
I remember, too, late that night, beating the bushes
with my clenched fist until my knuckles were gashed
and bleeding from the broken twigs. Then, sobbing
and raving in my anguish of mind, I went down to the
great building of stone. The big hall was dark, silent,
and deserted. I slipped on the uneven floor, and fell
over one of the malachite tables, almost breaking my
shin. I lit a match and went on past the dusty curtains,
of which I have told you.

"There I found a second great hall covered with
cushions, upon which, perhaps, a score or so of the
little people were sleeping. I have no doubt they found
my second appearance strange enough, coming suddenly out of the quiet darkness with inarticulate noises
and the splutter and flare of a match. For they had
forgotten about matches. 'Where is my Time Machine?' I began, bawling like an angry child, laying
hands upon them and shaking them up together. It
must have been very queer to them. Some laughed,
most of them looked sorely frightened. When I saw
them standing round me, it came into my head that I
was doing as foolish a thing as it was possible for me
to do under the circumstances, in trying to revive the
sensation of fear. For, reasoning from their daylight
behaviour, I thought that fear must be forgotten.

"Abruptly, I dashed down the match, and, knocking
one of the people over in my course, went blundering
across the big dining-hall again, out under the moon-

light. I heard cries of terror and their little feet running and stumbling this way and that. I do not remember all I did as the moon crept up the sky. I suppose it was the unexpected nature of my loss that maddened me. I felt hopelessly cut off from my own kind—a strange animal in an unknown world. I must have raved to and fro, screaming and crying upon God and Fate. I have a memory of horrible fatigue, as the long night of despair wore away; of looking in this impossible place and that; of groping among moonlit ruins and touching strange creatures in the black shadows; at last, of lying on the ground near the sphinx and weeping with absolute wretchedness. I had nothing left but misery. Then I slept, and when I woke again it was full day, and a couple of sparrows were hopping round me on the turf within reach of my arm.

"I sat up in the freshness of the morning, trying to remember how I had got there, and why I had such a profound sense of desertion and despair. Then things came clear in my mind. With the plain, reasonable daylight, I could look my circumstances fairly in the face. I saw the wild folly of my frenzy overnight, and I could reason with myself. 'Suppose the worst?' I said. 'Suppose the machine altogether lost—perhaps destroyed? It behoves me to be calm and patient, to learn the way of the people, to get a clear idea of the method of my loss, and the means of getting materials and tools; so that in the end, perhaps, I may make another.' That would be my only hope, perhaps, but better than despair. And, after all, it was a beautiful and curious world.

"But probably, the machine had only been taken away. Still, I must be calm and patient, find its hiding-place, and recover it by force or cunning. And with that I scrambled to my feet and looked about me, wondering where I could bathe. I felt weary, stiff, and

travel-soiled. The freshness of the morning made me
desire an equal freshness. I had exhausted my emotion. Indeed, as I went about my business, I found
myself wondering at my intense excitement overnight.
I made a careful examination of the ground about the
little lawn. I wasted some time in futile questionings,
conveyed, as well as I was able, to such of the little
people as came by. They all failed to understand my
gestures; some were simply stolid, some thought it was
a jest and laughed at me. I had the hardest task in
the world to keep my hands off their pretty laughing
faces. It was a foolish impulse, but the devil begotten
of fear and blind anger was ill curbed and still eager to
take advantage of my perplexity. The turf gave better
counsel. I found a groove ripped in it, about midway
between the pedestal of the sphinx and the marks of
my feet where, on arrival, I had struggled with the
overturned machine. There were other signs of re-
moval about, with queer narrow footprints like those
I could imagine made by a sloth. This directed my
closer attention to the pedestal. It was, as I think I
have said, of bronze. It was not a mere block, but
highly decorated with deep framed panels on either
side. I went and rapped at these. The pedestal was
hollow. Examining the panels with care I found them
discontinuous with the frames. There were no handles
or keyholes, but possibly the panels, if they were
doors, as I supposed, opened from within. It took no
very great mental effort to infer that my Time Machine was inside that pedestal. But how it got there
was a different problem.

"I saw the heads of two orange-clad people coming
through the bushes and under some blossom-covered
apple-trees towards me. I turned smiling to them and
beckoned them to me. They came, and then, pointing
to the bronze pedestal, I tried to intimate my wish to

open it. But at my first gesture towards this they behaved very oddly. I don't know how to convey their expression to you. Suppose you were to use a grossly improper gesture to a delicate-minded woman—it is how she would look. They went off as if they had received the last possible insult. I tried a sweet-looking little chap in white next, with exactly the same result. Somehow, his manner made me feel ashamed of myself. But, as you know, I wanted the Time Machine, and I tried him once more. As he turned off, like the others, my temper got the better of me. In three strides I was after him, had him by the loose part of his robe round the neck, and began dragging him towards the sphinx. Then I saw the horror and repugnance of his face, and all of a sudden I let him go.

"But I was not beaten yet. I banged with my fist at the bronze panels. I thought I heard something stir inside—to be explicit, I thought I heard a sound like a chuckle—but I must have been mistaken. Then I got a big pebble from the river, and came and hammered till I had flattened a coil in the decorations, and the verdigris came off in powdery flakes. The delicate little people must have heard me hammering in gusty outbreaks a mile away on either hand, but nothing came of it. I saw a crowd of them upon the slopes, looking furtively at me. At last, hot and tired, I sat down to watch the place. But I was too restless to watch long; I am too Occidental for a long vigil. I could work at a problem for years, but to wait inactive for twenty-four hours—that is another matter.

"I got up after a time, and began walking aimlessly through the bushes towards the hill again. 'Patience,' said I to myself. 'If you want your machine again you must leave that sphinx alone. If they mean to take your machine away, it's little good your wrecking their bronze panels, and if they don't, you will get it back

as soon as you can ask for it. To sit among all those
unknown things before a puzzle like that is hopeless.
That way lies monomania. Face this world. Learn its
ways, watch it, be careful of too hasty guesses at its
meaning. In the end you will find clues to it all.' Then
suddenly the humour of the situation came into my
mind: the thought of the years I had spent in study
and toil to get into the future age, and now my passion
of anxiety to get out of it. I had made myself the most
complicated and the most hopeless trap that ever a
man devised. Although it was at my own expense, I
could not help myself. I laughed aloud.

"Going through the big palace, it seemed to me that
the little people avoided me. It may have been my
fancy, or it may have had something to do with my
hammering at the gates of bronze. Yet I felt tolerably
sure of the avoidance. I was careful, however, to show
no concern and to abstain from any pursuit of them,
and in the course of a day or two things got back to
the old footing. I made what progress I could in the
language, and in addition I pushed my explorations
here and there. Either I missed some subtle point, or
their language was excessively simple—almost exclu-
sively composed of concrete substantives and verbs.
There seemed to be few, if any, abstract terms, or
little use of figurative language. Their sentences were
usually simple and of two words, and I failed to convey or understand any but the simplest propositions.
I determined to put the thought of my Time Machine
and the mystery of the bronze doors under the sphinx
as much as possible in a corner of memory, until my
growing knowledge would lead me back to them in a
natural way. Yet a certain feeling, you may understand, tethered me in a circle of a few miles round the
point of my arrival.

"So far as I could see, all the world displayed the

same exuberant richness as the Thames valley. From every hill I climbed I saw the same abundance of splendid buildings, endlessly varied in material and style, the same clustering thickets of evergreens, the same blossom-laden trees and tree-ferns. Here and there water shone like silver, and beyond, the land rose into blue undulating hills, and so faded into the serenity of the sky. A peculiar feature, which presently attracted my attention, was the presence of certain circular wells, several, as it seemed to me, of a very great depth. One lay by the path up the hill, which I had followed during my first walk. Like the others, it was rimmed with bronze, curiously wrought, and protected by a little cupola from the rain. Sitting by the side of these wells, and peering down into the shafted darkness, I could see no gleam of water, nor could I start any reflection with a lighted match. But in all of them I heard a certain sound: a thud—thud—thud, like the beating of some big engine; and I discovered, from the flaring of my matches, that a steady current of air set down the shafts. Further, I threw a scrap of paper into the throat of one, and, instead of fluttering slowly down, it was at once sucked swiftly out of sight.

"After a time, too, I came to connect these wells with tall towers standing here and there upon the slopes; for above them there was often just such a flicker in the air as one sees on a hot day above a sun-scorched beach. Putting things together, I reached a strong suggestion of an extensive system of subterranean ventilation, whose true import it was difficult to imagine. I was at first inclined to associate it with the sanitary apparatus of these people. It was an obvious conclusion, but it was absolutely wrong.

"And here I must admit that I learned very little of drains and bells and modes of conveyance, and the like conveniences, during my time in this real future. In some of these visions of Utopias and coming times which I have read, there is a vast amount of detail about building, and social arrangements, and so forth. But while such details are easy enough to obtain when the whole world is contained in one's imagination, they are altogether inaccessible to a real traveller amid such realities as I found here. Conceive the tale of London which a negro, fresh from Central Africa, would take back to his tribe! What would he know of railway companies, of social movements, of telephone and telegraph wires, of the Parcels Delivery Company, and postal orders and the like? Yet we, at least, should be willing enough to explain these things to him! And even of what he knew, how much could he make his untravelled friend either apprehend or believe? Then, think how narrow the gap between a negro and a white man of our own times, and how wide the interval between myself and these of the Golden Age! I was sensible of much which was unseen, and which contributed to my comfort; but save for a general impression of automatic organization, I fear I can convey very little of the difference to your mind.

"In the matter of sepulture, for instance, I could see no signs of crematoria nor anything suggestive of tombs. But it occurred to me that, possibly, there might be cemeteries (or crematoria) somewhere beyond the range of my explorings. This, again, was a question I deliberately put to myself, and my curiosity was at first entirely defeated upon the point. The thing puzzled me, and I was led to make a further remark, which puzzled me still more: that aged and infirm among this people there were none.

"I must confess that my satisfaction with my first theories of an automatic civilization and a decadent humanity did not long endure. Yet I could think of

no other. Let me put my difficulties. The several big
palaces I had explored were mere living places, great
dining-halls and sleeping apartments. I could find no
machinery, no appliances of any kind. Yet these people were clothed in pleasant fabrics that must at times
need renewal, and their sandals, though undecorated,
were fairly complex specimens of metalwork. Somehow such things must be made. And the little people
displayed no vestige of a creative tendency. There
were no shops, no workshops, no sign of importations
among them. They spent all their time in playing gently, in bathing in the river, in making love in a half-
playful fashion, in eating fruit and sleeping. I could
not see how things were kept going.

"Then, again, about the Time Machine: something,
I knew not what, had taken it into the hollow pedestal
of the White Sphinx. *Why?* For the life of me I could
not imagine. Those waterless wells, too, those flickering pillars. I felt I lacked a clue. I felt—how shall I
put it? Suppose you found an inscription, with sentences here and there in excellent plain English, and in-
terpolated therewith, others made up of words, of
letters even, absolutely unknown to you? Well, on the
third day of my visit, that was how the world of Eight
Hundred and Two Thousand Seven Hundred and One
presented itself to me!

"That day, too, I made a friend—of a sort. It happened that, as I was watching some of the little people
bathing in a shallow, one of them was seized with
cramp and began drifting downstream. The main current ran rather swiftly, but not too strongly for even
a moderate swimmer. It will give you an idea, therefore, of the strange deficiency in these creatures, when
I tell you that none made the slightest attempt to rescue the weakly crying little thing which was drowning
before their eyes. When I realized this, I hurriedly

slipped off my clothes, and, wading in at a point lower down, I caught the poor mite and drew her safe to land. A little rubbing of the limbs soon brought her round, and I had the satisfaction of seeing she was all right before I left her. I had got to such a low estimate of her kind that I did not expect any gratitude from her. In that, however, I was wrong.

"This happened in the morning. In the afternoon I met my little woman, as I believe it was, as I was returning towards my centre from an exploration, and she received me with cries of delight and presented me with a big garland of flowers—evidently made for me and me alone. The thing took my imagination. Very possibly I had been feeling desolate. At any rate I did my best to display my appreciation of the gift. We were soon seated together in a little stone arbour, engaged in conversation, chiefly of smiles. The creature's friendliness affected me exactly as a child's might have done. We passed each other flowers, and she kissed my hands. I did the same to hers. Then I tried talk, and found that her name was Weena, which, though I don't know what it meant, somehow seemed appropriate enough. That was the beginning of a queer friendship which lasted a week, and ended—as I will tell you!

"She was exactly like a child. She wanted to be with me always. She tried to follow me every where, and on my next journey out and about it went to my heart to tire her down, and leave her at last, exhausted and calling after me rather plaintively. But the problems of the world had to be mastered. I had not, I said to myself, come into the future to carry on a miniature flirtation. Yet her distress when I left her was very great, her expostulations at the parting were sometimes frantic, and I think, altogether, I had as much trouble as comfort from her devotion. Nevertheless she was, somehow, a very great comfort. I thought it was mere childish affection that made her cling to me. Until it was too late, I did not clearly know what I had inflicted upon her when I left her. Nor until it was too late did I clearly understand what she was to me. For, by merely seeming fond of me, and showing in her weak, futile way that she cared for me, the little doll of a creature presently gave my return to the neighbourhood of the White Sphinx almost the feeling of coming home; and I would watch for her tiny figure of white and gold so soon as I came over the hill.

"It was from her, too, that I learned that fear had not yet left the world. She was fearless enough in the daylight, and she had the oddest confidence in me; for once, in a foolish moment, I made threatening grimaces at her, and she simply laughed at them. But she dreaded the dark, dreaded shadows, dreaded black things. Darkness to her was the one thing dreadful. It was a singularly passionate emotion, and it set me thinking and observing. I discovered then, among other things, that these little people gathered into the great houses after dark, and slept in droves. To enter upon them without a light was to put them into a tumult of apprehension. I never found one out of doors, or one sleeping alone within doors, after dark. Yet I was still such a blockhead that I missed the lesson of that fear, and in spite of Weena's distress I insisted upon sleeping away from these slumbering multitudes.

"It troubled her greatly, but in the end her odd affection for me triumphed, and for five of the nights of our acquaintance, including the last night of all, she slept with her head pillowed on my arm. But my story slips away from me as I speak of her. It must have been the night before her rescue that I was awakened about dawn. I had been restless, dreaming most disagreeably that I was drowned, and that sea-anemones were feeling over my face with their soft palps. I woke with a start, and with an odd fancy that some greyish animal had just rushed out of the chamber. I tried to get to sleep again, but I felt restless and uncomfortable. It was that dim grey hour when things are just creeping out of darkness, when everything is colourless and clear cut, and yet unreal. I got up, and went down into the great hall, and so out upon the flagstones in front of the palace. I thought I would make a virtue of necessity, and see the sunrise.

"The moon was setting, and the dying moonlight and the first pallor of dawn were mingled in a ghastly half-light. The bushes were inky black, the ground a sombre grey, the sky colourless and cheerless. And up the hill I thought I could see ghosts. Three several times, as I scanned the slope, I saw white figures. Twice I fancied I saw a solitary white, ape-like creature running rather quickly up the hill, and once near the ruins I saw a leash of them carrying some dark body. They moved hastily. I did not see what became of them. It seemed that they vanished among the bushes. The dawn was still indistinct, you must understand. I was feeling that chill, uncertain, early-morning feeling you may have known. I doubted my eyes.

"As the eastern sky grew brighter, and the light of the day came on and its vivid colouring returned upon the world once more, I scanned the view keenly. But I saw no vestige of my white figures. They were mere creatures of the half-light. 'They must have been ghosts,' I said; 'I wonder whence they dated.' For a queer notion of Grant Allen's came into my head, and amused me. If each generation die and leave ghosts, he argued, the world at last will get overcrowded with them. On that theory they would have grown innumerable some Eight Hundred Thousand Years hence, and it was no great wonder to see four at once. But the jest was unsatisfying, and I was thinking of these figures all the morning, until Weena's rescue drove them out of my head. I associated them in some indefinite way with the white animal I had startled in my first passionate search for the Time Machine. But Weena was a pleasant substitute. Yet all the same, they were soon destined to take far deadlier possession of my mind.

"I think I have said how much hotter than our own was the weather of this Golden Age. I cannot account for it. It may be that the sun was hotter, or the earth nearer the sun. It is usual to assume that the sun will go on cooling steadily in the future. But people, unfamiliar with such speculations as those of the younger Darwin, forget that the planets must ultimately fall back one by one into the parent body. As these catastrophes occur, the sun will blaze with renewed energy; and it may be that some inner planet had suffered this fate. Whatever the reason, the fact remains that the sun was very much hotter than we know it.

"Well, one very hot morning—my fourth, I think— as I was seeking shelter from the heat and glare in a colossal ruin near the great house where I slept and fed, there happened this strange thing: Clambering among these heaps of masonry, I found a narrow gallery, whose end and side windows were blocked by fallen masses of stone. By contrast with the brilliancy outside, it seemed at first impenetrably dark to me. I entered it groping, for the change from light to blackness made spots of colour swim before me. Suddenly I halted spellbound. A pair of eyes, luminous by reflection against the daylight without, was watching me out of the darkness.

"The old instinctive dread of wild beasts came upon me. I clenched my hands and steadfastly looked into the glaring eyeballs. I was afraid to turn. Then the thought of the absolute security in which humanity appeared to be living came to my mind. And then I remembered that strange terror of the dark. Overcoming my fear to some extent, I advanced a step and spoke. I will admit that my voice was harsh and ill-controlled. I put out my hand and touched something soft. At once the eyes darted sideways, and something white ran past me. I turned with my heart in my mouth, and saw a queer little ape-like figure, its head held down in a peculiar manner, running across the sunlit space behind me. It blundered against a block of granite, staggered aside, and in a moment was hidden in a black shadow beneath another pile of ruined masonry.

"My impression of it is, of course, imperfect; but I know it was a dull white, and had strange large greyish-red eyes; also that there was flaxen hair on its head and down its back. But, as I say, it went too fast for me to see distinctly. I cannot even say whether it ran on all-fours, or only with its forearms held very low. After an instant's pause I followed it into the second heap of ruins. I could not find it at first; but, after a time in the profound obscurity, I came upon one of those round well-like openings of which I have told you, half closed by a fallen pillar. A sudden thought came to me. Could this Thing have vanished down the shaft? I lit a match, and, looking down, I saw a small, white, moving creature, with large bright eyes which regarded me steadfastly as it retreated. It made me shudder. It was so like a human spider! It was clambering down the wall, and now I saw for the first time a number of metal foot and hand rests forming a kind of ladder down the shaft. Then the light burned my fingers and fell out of my hand, going out as it dropped, and when I had lit another the little monster had disappeared.

"I do not know how long I sat peering down that well. It was not for some time that I could succeed in persuading myself that the thing I had seen was human. But, gradually, the truth dawned on me: that Man had not remained one species, but had differentiated into two distinct animals: that my graceful children of the Upper-world were not the sole descendants of our generation, but that this bleached, obscene, nocturnal Thing, which had flashed before me, was also heir to all the ages.

"I thought of the flickering pillars and of my theory of an underground ventilation. I began to suspect their true import. And what, I wondered, was this Lemur doing in my scheme of a perfectly balanced organization? How was it related to the indolent serenity of the beautiful Upper-worlders? And what was hidden down there, at the foot of that shaft? I sat upon the edge of the well telling myself that, at any rate, there was nothing to fear, and that there I must descend for the solution of my difficulties. And withal I was absolutely afraid to go! As I hesitated, two of the beautiful Upper-world people came running in their amorous sport across the daylight in the shadow. The male pursued the female, flinging flowers at her as he ran.

"They seemed distressed to find me, my arm against the overturned pillar, peering down the well. Apparently it was considered bad form to remark these apertures; for when I pointed to this one, and tried to frame a question about it in their tongue, they were still more visibly distressed and turned away. But they were interested by my matches, and I struck some to amuse them. I tried them again about the well, and again I failed. So presently I left them, meaning to go back to Weena, and see what I could get from her. But my mind was already in revolution; my guesses and impressions were slipping and sliding to a new adjustment. I had now a clue to the import of these wells, to the ventilating towers, to the mystery of the ghosts; to say nothing of a hint at the meaning of the bronze gates and the fate of the Time Machine! And very vaguely there came a suggestion towards the solution of the economic problem that had puzzled me.

"Here was the new view. Plainly, this second species of Man was subterranean. There were three circumstances in particular which made me think that its rare emergence above ground was the outcome of a long-continued underground habit. In the first place, there was the bleached look common in most animals that live largely in the dark—the white fish of the Kentucky caves, for instance. Then, those large eyes, with that capacity for reflecting light, are common features of nocturnal things—witness the owl and the cat. And last of all, that evident confusion in the sunshine, that hasty yet fumbling awkward flight towards dark shadow, and that peculiar carriage of the head while in the light—all reinforced the theory of an extreme sensitiveness of the retina.

"Beneath my feet, then, the earth must be tunnelled enormously, and these tunnellings were the habitat of the new race. The presence of ventilating shafts and wells along the hill slopes—everywhere, in fact, except along the river valley— showed how universal were its ramifications. What so natural, then, as to assume that it was in this artificial Under-world that such work as was necessary to the comfort of the daylight race was done? The notion was so plausible that I at once accepted it, and went on to assume the how of this splitting of the human species. I dare say you will anticipate the shape of my theory; though, for myself, I very soon felt that it fell far short of the truth.

"At first, proceeding from the problems of our own

age, it seemed clear as daylight to me that the gradual widening of the present merely temporary and social difference between the Capitalist and the Labourer, was the key to the whole position. No doubt it will seem grotesque enough to you—and wildly incredible!—and yet even now there are existing circumstances to point that way. There is a tendency to utilize underground space for the less ornamental purposes of civilization; there is the Metropolitan Railway in London, for instance, there are new electric railways, there are subways, there are underground workrooms and restaurants, and they increase and multiply. Evidently, I thought, this tendency had increased till Industry had gradually lost its birthright in the sky. I mean that it had gone deeper and deeper into larger and ever larger underground factories, spending a still-increasing amount of its time therein, till, in the end—! Even now, does not an East-end worker live in such artificial conditions as practically to be cut off from the natural surface of the earth?

"Again, the exclusive tendency of richer people—due, no doubt, to the increasing refinement of their education, and the widening gulf between them and the rude violence of the poor—is already leading to the closing, in their interest, of considerable portions of the surface of the land. About London, for instance, perhaps half the prettier country is shut in against intrusion. And this same widening gulf—which is due to the length and expense of the higher educational process and the increased facilities for and temptations towards refined habits on the part of the rich—will make that exchange between class and class, that promotion by intermarriage which at present retards the splitting of our species along lines of social stratification, less and less frequent. So, in the end, above ground you must have the Haves, pursuing pleasure and comfort and beauty, and below ground the Have-nots, the Workers getting continually adapted to the conditions of their labour. Once they were there, they would no doubt have to pay rent, and not a little of it, for the ventilation of their caverns; and if they refused, they would starve or be suffocated for arrears. Such of them as were so constituted as to be miserable and rebellious would die; and, in the end, the balance being permanent, the survivors would become as well adapted to the conditions of underground life, and as happy in their way, as the Upper-world people were to theirs. As it seemed to me, the refined beauty and the etiolated pallor followed naturally enough.

"The great triumph of Humanity I had dreamed of took a different shape in my mind. It had been no such triumph of moral education and general co-operation as I had imagined. Instead, I saw a real aristocracy, armed with a perfected science and working to a logical conclusion the industrial system of today. Its triumph had not been simply a triumph over Nature, but a triumph over Nature and the fellow-man. This, I must warn you, was my theory at the time. I had no convenient cicerone in the pattern of the Utopian books. My explanation may be absolutely wrong. I still think it is the most plausible one. But even on this supposition the balanced civilization that was at last attained must have long since passed its zenith, and was now far fallen into decay. The too-perfect security of the Upper-worlders had led them to a slow movement of degeneration, to a general dwindling in size, strength, and intelligence. That I could see clearly enough already. What had happened to the Undergrounders I did not yet suspect; but from what I had seen of the 'Morlocks'—that, by the by, was the name by which these creatures were called—I could imagine that the modification of the human type was even far more profound than among the 'Eloi,' the beautiful race that I already knew.

"Then came troublesome doubts. Why had the Morlocks taken my Time Machine? For I felt sure it was they who had taken it. Why, too, if the Eloi were masters, could they not restore the machine to me? And why were they so terribly afraid of the dark? I proceeded, as I have said, to question Weena about this Under-world, but here again I was disappointed. At first she would not understand my questions, and presently she refused to answer them. She shivered as though the topic was unendurable. And when I pressed her, perhaps a little harshly, she burst into tears. They were the only tears, except my own, I ever saw in that Golden Age. When I saw them I ceased abruptly to trouble about the Morlocks, and was only concerned in banishing these signs of the human inheritance from Weena's eyes. And very soon she was smiling and clapping her hands, while I solemnly burned a match.

6

"IT MAY SEEM odd to you, but it was two days before I could follow up the new-found clue in what was manifestly the proper way. I felt a peculiar shrinking from those pallid bodies. They were just the half-bleached colour of the worms and things one sees preserved in spirit in a zoological museum. And they were filthily cold to the touch. Probably my shrinking was largely due to the sympathetic influence of the Eloi, whose disgust of the Morlocks I now began to appreciate.

"The next night I did not sleep well. Probably my health was a little disordered. I was oppressed with perplexity and doubt. Once or twice I had a feeling of intense fear for which I could perceive no definite reason. I remember creeping noiselessly into the great hall where the little people were sleeping in the moonlight—that night Weena was among them—and feeling reassured by their presence. It occurred to me even then, that in the course of a few days the moon must pass through its last quarter, and the nights grow dark, when the appearances of these unpleasant creatures from below, these whitened Lemurs, this new vermin that had replaced the old, might be more abundant. And on both these days I had the restless feeling of one who shirks an inevitable duty. I felt assured that the Time Machine was only to be recovered by boldly penetrating these underground mysteries. Yet I could not face the mystery. If only I had had a companion it would have been different. But I was so horribly alone, and even to clamber down into the darkness of the well appalled me. I don't know if you will understand my feeling, but I never felt quite safe at my back.

"It was this restlessness, this insecurity, perhaps, that drove me further and further afield in my exploring expeditions. Going to the south-westward towards the rising country that is now called Combe Wood, I observed far off, in the direction of nineteenth-century Banstead, a vast green structure, different in character from any I had hitherto seen. It was larger than the largest of the palaces or ruins I knew, and the façade had an Oriental look: the face of it having the lustre, as well as the pale-green tint, a kind of bluish-green, of a certain type of Chinese porcelain. This difference in aspect suggested a difference in use, and I was minded to push on and explore. But the day was growing late, and I had come upon the sight of the place after a long and tiring circuit; so I resolved to hold over the adventure for the following day, and I returned to the welcome and the caresses of little Weena. But next morning I perceived clearly enough that my curiosity regarding the Palace of Green Porcelain was a piece of self-deception, to enable me to shirk, by another day, an experience I dreaded. I resolved I would make the descent without further waste of time, and started out in the early morning towards a well near the ruins of granite and aluminium.

"Little Weena ran with me. She danced beside me to the well, but when she saw me lean over the mouth and look downward, she seemed strangely disconcerted. 'Good-bye, little Weena,' I said, kissing her;

and then, putting her down, I began to feel over the parapet for the climbing hooks. Rather hastily, I may as well confess, for I feared my courage might leak away! At first she watched me in amazement. Then she gave a most piteous cry, and, running to me, she began to pull at me with her little hands. I think her opposition nerved me rather to proceed. I shook her off, perhaps a little roughly, and in another moment I was in the throat of the well. I saw her agonized face over the parapet, and smiled to reassure her. Then I had to look down at the unstable hooks to which I clung.

"I had to clamber down a shaft of perhaps two hundred yards. The descent was effected by means of metallic bars projecting from the sides of the well, and these being adapted to the needs of a creature much smaller and lighter than myself, I was speedily cramped and fatigued by the descent. And not simply fatigued! One of the bars bent suddenly under my weight, and almost swung me off into the blackness beneath. For a moment I hung by one hand, and after that experience I did not dare to rest again. Though my arms and back were presently acutely painful, I went on clambering down the sheer descent with as quick a motion as possible. Glancing upward, I saw the aperture, a small blue disk, in which a star was visible, while little Weena's head showed as a round black projection. The thudding sound of a machine below grew louder and more oppressive. Everything save that little disk above was profoundly dark, and when I looked up again Weena had disappeared.

"I was in an agony of discomfort. I had some thought of trying to go up the shaft again, and leave the Under-world alone. But even while I turned this over in my mind I continued to descend. At last, with intense relief, I saw dimly coming up, a foot to the right of me, a slender loophole in the wall. Swinging myself in, I found it was the aperture of a narrow horizontal tunnel in which I could lie down and rest. It was not too soon. My arms ached, my back was cramped, and I was trembling with the prolonged terror of a fall. Besides this, the unbroken darkness had had a distressing effect upon my eyes. The air was full of the throb and hum of machinery pumping air down the shaft.

"I do not know how long I lay. I was roused by a soft hand touching my face. Starting up in the darkness I snatched at my matches and, hastily striking one, I saw three stooping white creatures similar to the one I had seen above ground in the ruin, hastily retreating before the light. Living, as they did, in what appeared to me impenetrable darkness, their eyes were abnormally large and sensitive, just as are the pupils of the abysmal fishes, and they reflected the light in the same way. I have no doubt they could see me in that rayless obscurity, and they did not seem to have any fear of me apart from the light. But, so soon as I struck a match in order to see them, they fled incontinently, vanishing into dark gutters and tunnels, from which their eyes glared at me in the strangest fashion.

"I tried to call to them, but the language they had was apparently different from that of the Over-world people; so that I was needs left to my own unaided efforts, and the thought of flight before exploration was even then in my mind. But I said to myself, 'You are in for it now,' and, feeling my way along the tunnel, I found the noise of machinery grow louder. Presently the walls fell away from me, and I came to a large open space, and striking another match, saw that I had entered a vast arched cavern, which stretched into utter darkness beyond the range of my light. The view I had of it was as much as one could see in the burning of a match.

"Necessarily my memory is vague. Great shapes like big machines rose out of the dimness, and cast grotesque black shadows, in which dim spectral Morlocks sheltered from the glare. The place, by the by, was very stuffy and oppressive, and the faint halitus of freshly shed blood was in the air. Some way down the central vista was a little table of white metal, laid with what seemed a meal. The Morlocks at any rate were carnivorous! Even at the time, I remember wondering what large animal could have survived to furnish the red joint I saw. It was all very indistinct: the heavy smell, the big unmeaning shapes, the obscene figures lurking in the shadows, and only waiting for the darkness to come at me again! Then the match burned down, and stung my fingers, and fell, a wriggling red spot in the blackness.

"I have thought since how particularly ill-equipped I was for such an experience. When I had started with the Time Machine, I had started with the absurd assumption that the men of the Future would certainly be infinitely ahead of ourselves in all their appliances. I had come without arms, without medicine, without anything to smoke—at times I missed tobacco frightfully—even without enough matches. If only I had thought of a Kodak! I could have flashed that glimpse of the Under-world in a second, and examined it at leisure. But, as it was, I stood there with only the weapons and the powers that Nature had endowed me with—hands, feet, and teeth; these, and four safety-matches that still remained to me.

"I was afraid to push my way in among all this machinery in the dark, and it was only with my last glimpse of light I discovered that my store of matches had run low. It had never occurred to me until that moment that there was any need to economize them, and I had wasted almost half the box in astonishing the Upper-worlders, to whom fire was a novelty. Now, as I say, I had four left, and while I stood in the dark, a hand touched mine, lank fingers came feeling over my face, and I was sensible of a peculiar unpleasant odour. I fancied I heard the breathing of a crowd of those dreadful little beings about me. I felt the box of matches in my hand being gently disengaged, and other hands behind me plucking at my clothing. The sense of these unseen creatures examining me was indescribably unpleasant. The sudden realization of my ignorance of their ways of thinking and doing came home to me very vividly in the darkness. I shouted at them as loudly as I could. They started away, and then I could feel them approaching me again. They clutched at me more boldly, whispering odd sounds to each other. I shivered violently, and shouted again—rather discordantly. This time they were not so seriously alarmed, and they made a queer laughing noise as they came back at me. I will confess I was horribly frightened. I determined to stroke another match and escape under the protection of its glare. I did so, and eking out the flicker with a scrap of paper from my pocket, I made good my retreat to the narrow tunnel. But I had scarce entered this when my light was blown out, and in the blackness I could hear the Morlocks rustling like wind among leaves, and pattering like the rain, as they hurried after me.

"In a moment I was clutched by several hands, and there was no mistaking that they were trying to haul me back. I struck another light, and waved it in their dazzled faces. You can scarce imagine how nauseatingly inhuman they looked—those pale, chinless faces and great, lidless, pinkish-grey eyes!—as they stared in their blindness and bewilderment. But I did not stay to look, I promise you: I retreated again, and when my second match had ended, I struck my third. It had almost burned through when I reached the opening into the shaft. I lay down on the edge, for the throb of the great pump below made me giddy. Then I felt sideways for the projecting hooks, and, as I did so, my feet were grasped from behind, and I was violently tugged backward. I lit my last match . . . and it incontinently went out. But I had my hand on the climbing bars now, and, kicking violently, I disengaged myself from the clutches of the Morlocks and was speedily clambering up the shaft, while they stayed peering and blinking up at me: all but one little wretch who followed me for some way, and wellnigh secured my boot as a trophy.

"That climb seemed interminable to me. With the last twenty or thirty feet of it a deadly nausea came upon me. I had the greatest difficulty in keeping my hold. The last few yards was a frightful struggle against this faintness. Several times my head swam, and I felt all the sensations of falling. At last, however, I got over the well-mouth somehow, and staggered out of the ruin into the blinding sunlight. I fell upon my face. Even the soil smelt sweet and clean. Then I remember Weena kissing my hands and ears, and the voices of others among the Eloi. Then, for a time, I was insensible.

7

"Now, indeed, I seemed in a worse case than before. Hitherto, except during my night's anguish at the loss of the Time Machine, I had felt a sustaining hope of ultimate escape, but that hope was staggered by these new discoveries. Hitherto I had merely thought myself impeded by the childish simplicity of the little people, and by some unknown forces which I had only to understand to overcome; but there was an altogether new element in the sickening quality of the Morlocks—a something inhuman and malign. Instinctively I loathed them. Before, I had felt as a man might feel who had fallen into a pit: my concern was with the pit and how to get out of it. Now I felt like a beast in a trap, whose enemy would come upon him soon.

"The enemy I dreaded may surprise you. It was the darkness of the new moon. Weena had put this into my head by some at first incomprehensible remarks about the Dark Nights. It was not now such a very difficult problem to guess what the coming Dark Nights might mean. The moon was on the wane: each night there was a longer interval of darkness. And I now understood to some slight degree at least the reason of the fear of the little Upper-world people for the dark. I wondered vaguely what foul villainy it might be that the Morlocks did under the new moon.

I felt pretty sure now that my second hypothesis was all wrong. The Upper-world people might once have been the favoured aristocracy, and the Morlocks their mechanical servants: but that had long since passed away. The two species that had resulted from the evolution of man were sliding down towards, or had already arrived at, an altogether new relationship. The Eloi, like the Carlovingian kings, had decayed to a mere beautiful futility. They still possessed the earth on sufferance: since the Morlocks, subterranean for innumerable generations, had come at last to find the daylit surface intolerable. And the Morlocks made their garments, I inferred, and maintained them in their habitual needs, perhaps through the survival of an old habit of service. They did it as a standing horse paws with his foot, or as a man enjoys killing animals in sport: because ancient and departed necessities had impressed it on the organism. But, clearly, the old order was already in part reversed. The Nemesis of the delicate ones was creeping on apace. Ages ago, thousands of generations ago, man had thrust his brother man out of the ease and the sunshine. And now that brother was coming back—changed! Already the Eloi had begun to learn one old lesson anew. They were becoming reacquainted with Fear. And suddenly there came into my head the memory of the meat I had seen in the Under-world. It seemed odd how it floated into my mind: not stirred up as it were by the current of my meditations, but coming in almost like a question from outside. I tried to recall the form of it. I had a vague sense of something familiar, but I could not tell what it was at the time.

"Still, however helpless the little people in the presence of their mysterious Fear, I was differently constituted. I came out of this age of ours, this ripe prime of the human race, where Fear does not paralyse and mystery has lost its terrors. I at least would defend myself. Without further delay I determined to make myself arms and a fastness where I might sleep. With that refuge as a base, I could face this strange world with some of that confidence I had lost in realizing to what creatures night by night I lay exposed. I felt I could never sleep again until my bed was secure from them. I shuddered with horror to think how they must already have examined me.

"I wandered during the afternoon along the valley of the Thames, but found nothing that commended itself to my mind as inaccessible. All the buildings and trees seemed easily practicable to such dexterous climbers as the Morlocks, to judge by their wells, must be. Then the tall pinnacle of the Palace of Green Porcelain and the polished gleam of its walls came back to my memory; and in the evening, taking Weena like a child upon my shoulder, I went up the hills towards the south-west. The distance, I had reckoned, was seven or eight miles, but it must have been nearer eighteen. I had first seen the place on a moist afternoon when distances are deceptively diminished. In addition, the heel of one of my shoes was loose, and a nail was working through the sole—they were comfortable old shoes I wore about indoors—so that I was lame. And it was already long past sunset when I came in sight of the palace, silhouetted black against the pale yellow of the sky.

"Weena had been hugely delighted when I began to carry her, but after a time she desired me to let her down, and ran along by the side of me, occasionally darting off on either hand to pick flowers to stick in my pockets. My pockets had always puzzled Weena, but at the last she had concluded that they were an eccentric kind of vase for floral decoration. At least she utilized them for that purpose. And that reminds me! In changing my jacket I found . . .''

The Time Traveller paused, put his hand into his pocket, and silently placed two withered flowers, not unlike very large white mallows, upon the little table. Then he resumed his narrative.

"As the hush of evening crept over the world and we proceeded over the hill crest towards Wimbledon, Weena grew tired and wanted to return to the house of grey stone. But I pointed out the distant pinnacles of the Palace of Green Porcelain to her, and contrived to make her understand that we were seeking a refuge there from her Fear. You know that great pause that comes upon things before the dusk? Even the breeze stops in the trees. To me there is always an air of expectation about that evening stillness. The sky was clear, remote, and empty save for a few horizontal bars far down in the sunset. Well, that night the expectation took the colour of my fears. In that darkling calm my senses seemed preternaturally sharpened. I fancied I could even feel the hollowness of the ground beneath my feet: could, indeed, almost see through it the Morlocks on their anthill going hither and thither and waiting for the dark. In my excitement I fancied that they would receive my invasion of their burrows as a declaration of war. And why had they taken my Time Machine?

"So we went on in the quiet, and the twilight deepened into night. The clear blue of the distance faded, and one star after another came out. The ground grew dim and the trees black. Weena's fears and her fatigue grew upon her. I took her in my arms and talked to her and caressed her. Then, as the darkness grew deeper, she put her arms round my neck, and, closing her eyes, tightly pressed her face against my shoulder.

So we went down a long slope into a valley, and there in the dimness I almost walked into a little river. This I waded, and went up on the opposite side of the valley, past a number of sleeping houses, and by a statue—a Faun, or some such figure, *minus* the head. Here too were acacias. So far I had seen nothing of the Morlocks, but it was yet early in the night, and the darker hours before the old moon rose were still to come.

"From the brow of the next hill I saw a thick wood spreading wide and black before me. I hesitated at this. I could see no end to it, either to the right or the left. Feeling tired—my feet, in particular, were very sore—I carefully lowered Weena from my shoulder as I halted, and sat down upon the turf. I could no longer see the Palace of Green Porcelain, and I was in doubt of my direction. I looked into the thickness of the wood and thought of what it might hide. Under that dense tangle of branches one would be out of sight of the stars. Even were there no other lurking danger—a danger I did not care to let my imagination loose upon—there would still be all the roots to stumble over and the tree-boles to strike against.

"I was very tired, too, after the excitements of the day; so I decided that I would not face it, but would pass the night upon the open hill.

"Weena, I was glad to find, was fast asleep. I carefully wrapped her in my jacket, and sat down beside her to wait for the moonrise. The hill-side was quiet and deserted, but from the black of the wood there came now and then a stir of living things. Above me shone the stars, for the night was very clear. I felt a certain sense of friendly comfort in their twinkling. All the old constellations had gone from the sky, however: that slow movement which is imperceptible in a hundred human lifetimes, had long since rearranged them in unfamiliar groupings. But the Milky Way, it seemed to me, was still the same tattered streamer of star-dust as of yore. Southward (as I judged it) was a very bright red star that was new to me; it was even more splendid than our own green Sirius. And amid all these scintillating points of light one bright planet shone kindly and steadily like the face of an old friend.

"Looking at these stars suddenly dwarfed my own troubles and all the gravities of terrestrial life. I thought of their unfathomable distance, and the slow inevitable drift of their movements out of the unknown past into the unknown future. I thought of the great precessional cycle that the pole of the earth describes. Only forty times had that silent revolution occurred during all the years that I had traversed. And during these few revolutions all the activity, all the traditions, the complex organizations, the nations, languages, literatures, aspirations, even the mere memory of Man as I knew him, had been swept out of existence. Instead were these frail creatures who had forgotten their high ancestry, and the white Things of which I went in terror. Then I thought of the Great Fear that was between the two species, and for the first time, with a sudden shiver, came the clear knowledge of what the meat I had seen might be. Yet it was too horrible! I looked at little Weena sleeping beside me, her face white and starlike under the stars, and forthwith dismissed the thought.

"Through that long night I held my mind off the Morlocks as well as I could, and whiled away the time by trying to fancy I could find signs of the old constellations in the new confusion. The sky kept very clear, except for a hazy cloud or so. No doubt I dozed at times. Then, as my vigil wore on, came a faintness in the eastward sky, like the reflection of some colourless fire, and the old moon rose, thin and peaked and white. And close behind, and overtaking it, and overflowing it, the dawn came, pale at first, and then growing pink and warm. No Morlocks had approached us. Indeed, I had seen none upon the hill that night. And in the confidence of renewed day it almost seemed to me that my fear had been unreasonable. I stood up and found my foot with the loose heel swollen at the ankle and painful under the heel so I sat down again, took off my shoes, and flung them away.

"I awakened Weena, and we went down into the wood, now green and pleasant instead of black and forbidding. We found some fruit wherewith to break our fast. We soon met others of the dainty ones, laughing and dancing in the sunlight as though there was no such thing in nature as the night. And then I thought once more of the meat that I had seen. I felt assured now of what it was, and from the bottom of my heart I pitied this last feeble rill from the great flood of humanity. Clearly, at some time in the Long-Ago of human decay the Morlocks' food had run short. Possibly they had lived on rats and such-like vermin. Even now man is far less discriminating and exclusive in his food than he was—far less than any monkey. His prejudice against human flesh is no deep-seated instinct. And so these inhuman sons of men——! I tried to look at the thing in a scientific spirit. After all, they were less human and more remote than our cannibal ancestors of three or four thousand years ago. And the intelligence that would have made this state of things a torment had gone. Why should I trouble myself? These Eloi were mere fatted cattle, which the ant-like Morlocks preserved and preyed upon—probably saw to the breeding of. And there was Weena dancing at my side!

"Then I tried to preserve myself from the horror

that was coming upon me, by regarding it as a rigorous punishment of human selfishness. Man had been content to live in ease and delight upon the labours of his fellow-man, had taken Necessity as his watchword and excuse, and in the fullness of time Necessity had come home to him. I even tried a Carlyle-like scorn of this wretched aristocracy in decay. But this attitude of mind was impossible. However great their intellectual degradation, the Eloi had kept too much of the human form not to claim my sympathy, and to make me perforce a sharer in their degradation and their Fear.

"I had at that time very vague ideas as to the course I should pursue. My first was to secure some safe place of refuge, and to make myself such arms of metal or stone as I could contrive. That necessity was immediate. In the next place, I hoped to procure some means of fire, so that I should have the weapon of a torch at hand, for nothing, I knew, would be more efficient against these Morlocks. Then I wanted to arrange some contrivance to break open the doors of bronze under the White Sphinx. I had in mind a battering-ram. I had a persuasion that if I could enter those doors and carry a blaze of light before me I should discover the Time Machine and escape. I could not imagine the Morlocks were strong enough to move it far away. Weena I had resolved to bring with me to our own time. And turning such schemes over in my mind, I pursued our way towards the building which my fancy had chosen as our dwelling.

8

"I FOUND the Palace of Green Porcelain, when we approached it about noon, deserted and falling into ruin. Only ragged vestiges of glass remained in its windows, and great sheets of the green facing had fallen away from the corroded metallic framework. It lay very high upon a turfy down, and looking north-eastward before I entered it, I was surprised to see a large estuary, or even creek, where I judged Wandsworth and Battersea must once have been. I thought then—though I never followed up the thought—of what might have happened, or might be happening, to the living things in the sea.

"The material of the Palace proved on examination to be indeed porcelain, and along the face of it I saw an inscription in some unknown character. I thought, rather foolishly, that Weena might help me to interpret this, but I only learned that the bare idea of writing had never entered her head. She always seemed to me, I fancy, more human than she was, perhaps because her affection was so human.

"Within the big valves of the door—which were open and broken—we found, instead of the customary hall, a long gallery lit by many side windows. At the first glance I was reminded of a museum. The tiled floor was thick with dust, and a remarkable array of miscellaneous objects was shrouded in the same grey covering. Then I perceived, standing strange and gaunt in the centre of the hall, what was clearly the lower part of a huge skeleton. I recognized by the oblique feet that it was some extinct creature after the fashion of the Megatherium. The skull and the upper bones lay beside it in the thick dust, and in one place, where rain-water had dropped through a leak in the roof, the thing itself had been worn away. Further in the gallery was the huge skeleton barrel of a Brontosaurus. My museum hypothesis was confirmed. Going towards the side I found what appeared to be sloping shelves, and clearing away the thick dust, I found the old familiar glass cases of our own time. But they must have been airtight to judge from the fair preservation of some of their contents.

"Clearly we stood among the ruins of some latter-day South Kensington! Here, apparently, was the Palaeontological Section, and a very splendid array of fossils it must have been, though the inevitable process of decay that had been staved off for a time, and had, through the extinction of bacteria and fungi, lost ninety-nine hundredths of its force, was nevertheless, with extreme sureness if with extreme slowness at work again upon all its treasures. Here and there I found traces of the little people in the shape of rare fossils broken to pieces or threaded in strings upon reeds. And the cases had in some instances been bodily removed—by the Morlocks as I judged. The place was very silent. The thick dust deadened our footsteps. Weena, who had been rolling a sea-urchin down the sloping glass of a case, presently came, as I stared about me, and very quietly took my hand and stood beside me.

"And at first I was so much surprised by this ancient monument of an intellectual age, that I gave no

thought to the possibilities it presented. Even my pre-
occupation about the Time Machine receded a little
from my mind.

"To judge from the size of the place, this Palace of
Green Porcelain had a great deal more in it than a
Gallery of Palaeontology; possibly historical galleries;
it might be, even a library! To me, at least in my
present circumstances, these would be vastly more in-
teresting than this spectacle of old-time geology in
decay. Exploring, I found another short gallery running transversely to the first. This appeared to be devoted to minerals, and the sight of a block of sulphur
set my mind running on gunpowder. But I could find
no saltpeter; indeed, no nitrates of any kind. Doubtless
they had deliquesced ages ago. Yet the sulphur hung
in my mind, and set up a train of thinking. As for the
rest of the contents of that gallery, though on the
whole they were the best preserved of all I saw, I had
little interest. I am no specialist in mineralogy, and I
went on down a very ruinous aisle running parallel to
the first hall I had entered. Apparently this section
had been devoted to natural history, but everything
had long since passed out of recognition. A few shrivelled and blackened vestiges of what had once been
stuffed animals, desiccated mummies in jars that had
once held spirit, a brown dust of departed plants: that
was all! I was sorry for that, because I should have
been glad to trace the patent readjustments by which
the conquest of animated nature had been attained.
Then we came to a gallery of simply colossal propor-
tions, but singularly ill-lit, the floor of it running downward at a slight angle from the end at which I entered.
At intervals white globes hung from the ceiling—many
of them cracked and smashed—which suggested that
originally the place had been artificially lit. Here I was
more in my element, for rising on either side of me

were the huge bulks of big machines, all greatly corroded and many broken down, but some still fairly complete. You know I have a certain weakness for mechanism, and I was inclined to linger among these; the more so as for the most part they had the interest of puzzles, and I could make only the vaguest guesses at what they were for. I fancied that if I could solve their puzzles I should find myself in possession of powers that might be of use against the Morlocks.

"Suddenly Weena came very close to my side. So suddenly that she startled me. Had it not been for her I do not think I should have noticed that the floor of the gallery sloped at all.[1] The end I had come in at was quite above ground, and was lit by rare slit-like windows. As you went down the length, the ground came up against these windows, until at last there was a pit like the 'area' of a London house before each, and only a narrow line of daylight at the top. I went slowly along, puzzling about the machines, and had been too intent upon them to notice the gradual diminution of the light, until Weena's increasing apprehensions drew my attention. Then I saw that the gallery ran down at last into a thick darkness. I hesitated, and then, as I looked round me, I saw that the dust was less abundant and its surface less even. Further away towards the dimness, it appeared to be broken by a number of small narrow footprints. My sense of the immediate presence of the Morlocks revived at that. I felt that I was wasting my time in this academic examination of machinery. I called to mind that it was already far advanced in the afternoon, and that I had still no weapon, no refuge, and no means of making a fire. And then down in the remote blackness of the

---

[1] It may be, of course, that the floor did not slope, but that the museum was built into the side of a hill.—ED.

gallery I heard a peculiar pattering, and the same odd noises I had heard down the well.

"I took Weena's hand. Then, struck with a sudden idea, I left her and turned to a machine from which projected a lever not unlike those in a signal-box. Clambering upon the stand, and grasping this lever in my hands, I put all my weight upon it sideways. Suddenly Weena, deserted in the central aisle, began to whimper. I had judged the strength of the lever pretty correctly, for it snapped after a minute's strain, and I rejoined her with a mace in my hand more than sufficient, I judged, for any Morlock skull I might encounter. And I longed very much to kill a Morlock or so. Very inhuman, you may think, to want to go killing one's own descendants! But it was impossible, somehow, to feel any humanity in the things. Only my disinclination to leave Weena, and a persuasion that if I began to slake my thirst for murder my Time Machine might suffer, restrained me from going straight down the gallery and killing the brutes I heard.

"Well, mace in one hand and Weena in the other, I went out of that gallery and into another and still larger one, which at the first glance reminded me of a military chapel hung with tattered flags. The brown and charred rags that hung from the sides of it, I presently recognized as the decaying vestiges of books. They had long since dropped to pieces, and every semblance of print had left them. But here and there were warped boards and cracked metallic clasps that told the tale well enough. Had I been a literary man I might, perhaps, have moralized upon the futility of all ambition. But as it was, the thing that struck me with keenest force was the enormous waste of labour to which this sombre wilderness of rotting paper testified. At the time I will confess that I thought chiefly of the *Philosophical Transactions* and my own seventeen papers upon physical optics.

"Then, going up a board staircase, we came to what may once have been a gallery of technical chemistry. And here I had not a little hope of useful discoveries. Except at one end where the roof had collapsed, this gallery was well preserved. I went eagerly to every unbroken case. And at last, in one of the really airtight cases, I found a box of matches. Very eagerly I tried them. They were perfectly good. They were not even damp. I turned to Weena. 'Dance,' I cried to her in her own tongue. For now I had a weapon indeed against the horrible creatures we feared. And so, in that derelict museum, upon the thick soft carpeting of dust, to Weena's huge delight, I solemnly performed a kind of composite dance, whistling *The Land of the Leal* as cheerfully as I could. In part it was a modest *cancan*, in part a step-dance, in part a skirt-dance (so far as my tail-coat permitted), and in part original. For I am naturally inventive, as you know.

"Now, I still think that for this box of matches to have escaped the wear of time for immemorial years was a most strange, as for me it was a most fortunate thing. Yet, oddly enough, I found a far unlikelier substance, and that was camphor. I found it in a sealed jar, that by chance, I suppose, had been really hermetically sealed. I fancied at first that it was paraffin wax, and smashed the glass accordingly. But the odour of camphor was unmistakable. In the universal decay this volatile substance had chanced to survive, perhaps through many thousands of centuries. It reminded me of a sepia painting I had once seen done from the ink of a fossil Belemnite that must have perished and become fossilized millions of years ago. I was about to throw it away, but I remembered that it was inflammable and burned with a good bright flame—was, in fact, an excellent candle—and I put it in my pocket. I found no explosives, however, nor any means of breaking down the bronze doors. As yet my iron crowbar was the most helpful thing I had chanced upon. Nevertheless I left that gallery greatly elated.

"I cannot tell you all the story of that long afternoon. It would require a great effort of memory to recall my explorations in at all the proper order. I remember a long gallery of rusting stands of arms, and how I hesitated between my crowbar and a hatchet or a sword. I could not carry both, however, and my bar of iron promised best against the bronze gates. There were numbers of guns, pistols, and rifles. The most were masses of rust, but many were of some new metal, and still fairly sound. But any cartridges or powder there may once have been had rotted into dust. One corner I saw was charred and shattered; perhaps, I thought, by an explosion among the specimens. In another place was a vast array of idols—Polynesian, Mexican, Grecian, Phoenician, every country on earth I should think. And here, yielding to an irresistible impulse, I wrote my name upon the nose of a steatite monster from South America that particularly took my fancy.

"As the evening drew on, my interest waned. I went through gallery after gallery, dusty, silent, often ruinous, the exhibits sometimes mere heaps of rust and lignite, sometimes fresher. In one place I suddenly found myself near the model of a tin-mine, and then by the merest accident I discovered, in an air-tight case, two dynamite cartridges! I shouted 'Eureka!' and smashed the case with joy. Then came a doubt. I hesitated. Then, selecting a little side gallery, I made my essay. I never felt such a disappointment as I did in waiting five, ten, fifteen minutes for an explosion that never came. Of course the things were dummies, as I might have guessed from their presence. I really believe that, had they not been so, I should have rushed off incontinently and blown Sphinx, bronze doors, and (as it proved) my chances of finding the Time Machine, all together into non-existence.

"It was after that, I think, that we came to a little open court within the palace. It was turfed, and had three fruit-trees. So we rested and refreshed ourselves. Towards sunset I began to consider our position. Night was creeping upon us, and my inaccessible hiding-place had still to be found. But that troubled me very little now. I had in my possession a thing that was, perhaps, the best of all defences against the Morlocks—I had matches! I had the camphor in my pocket, too, if a blaze were needed. It seemed to me that the best thing we could do would be to pass the night in the open, protected by a fire. In the morning there was the getting of the Time Machine. Towards that, as yet, I had only my iron mace. But now, with my growing knowledge, I felt very differently towards those bronze doors. Up to this, I had refrained from forcing them, largely because of the mystery on the other side. They had never impressed me as being very strong, and I hoped to find my bar of iron not altogether inadequate for the work.

9

''WE EMERGED from the palace while the sun was still in part above the horizon. I was determined to reach the White Sphinx early the next morning, and ere the dusk I purposed pushing through the woods that had stopped me on the previous journey. My plan was to go as far as possible that night, and then, building a fire, to sleep in the protection of its glare. Accordingly, as we went along I gathered any sticks or dried grass I saw, and presently had my arms full of such litter. Thus loaded, our progress was slower than I had anticipated, and besides Weena was tired. And I began to suffer from sleepiness too; so that it was full night before we reached the wood. Upon the shrubby hill of its edge Weena would have stopped, fearing the darkness before us; but a singular sense of impending calamity, that should indeed have served me as a warning, drove me onward. I had been without sleep for a night and two days, and I was feverish and irritable. I felt sleep coming upon me, and the Morlocks with it.

"While we hesitated, among the black bushes behind us, and dim against their blackness, I saw three crouching figures. There was scrub and long grass all about us, and I did not feel safe from their insidious approach. The forest, I calculated, was rather less than a mile across. If we could get through it to the bare hill-side, there, as it seemed to me, was an altogether safer resting-place; I thought that with my matches and my camphor I could contrive to keep my path illuminated through the woods. Yet it was evident that if I was to flourish matches with my hands I should have to abandon my firewood; so, rather reluctantly, I put it down. And then it came into my head that I would amaze our friends behind by lighting it. I was to discover the atrocious folly of this proceeding, but it came to my mind as an ingenious move for covering our retreat.

"I don't know if you have ever thought what a rare thing flame must be in the absence of man and in a temperate climate. The sun's heat is rarely strong enough to burn, even when it is focused by dewdrops, as is sometimes the case in more tropical districts. Lightning may blast and blacken, but it rarely gives rise to widespread fire. Decaying vegetation may occasionally smoulder with the heat of its fermentation, but this rarely results in flame. In this decadence, too, the art of fire-making had been forgotten on the earth. The red tongues that went licking up my heap of wood were an altogether new and strange thing to Weena.

"She wanted to run to it and play with it. I believe she would have cast herself into it had I not restrained her. But I caught her up, and, in spite of her struggles, plunged boldly before me into the wood. For a little way the glare of my fire lit the path. Looking back presently, I could see, through the crowded stems, that from my heap of sticks the blaze had spread to some bushes adjacent, and a curved line of fire was creeping up the grass of the hill. I laughed at that, and turned again to the dark trees before me. It was very black, and Weena clung to me convulsively, but there was still, as my eyes grew accustomed to the darkness, sufficient light for me to avoid the stems. Overhead it was simply black, except where a gap of remote blue sky shone down upon us here and there. I struck none of my matches because I had no hand free. Upon my left arm I carried my little one, in my right hand I had my iron bar.

"For some way I heard nothing but the crackling twigs under my feet, the faint rustle of the breeze above, and my own breathing and the throb of the blood-vessels in my ears. Then I seemed to know of a pattering about me. I pushed on grimly. The pattering grew more distinct, and then I caught the same queer sound and voices I had heard in the Underworld. There were evidently several of the Morlocks, and they were closing in upon me. Indeed, in another minute I felt a tug at my coat, then something at my arm. And Weena shivered violently, and became quite still.

"It was time for a match. But to get one I must put her down. I did so, and, as I fumbled with my pocket, a struggle began in the darkness about my knees, perfectly silent on her part and with the same peculiar cooing sounds from the Morlocks. Soft little hands, too, were creeping over my coat and back, touching even my neck. Then the match scratched and fizzed. I held it flaring, and saw the white backs of the Morlocks in flight amid the trees. I hastily took a lump of camphor from my pocket, and prepared to light it as soon as the match should wane. Then I looked at Weena. She was lying clutching my feet and quite motionless, with her face to the ground. With a sudden fright I stooped to her. She seemed scarcely to breathe. I lit the block of camphor and flung it to the ground, and as it split and flared up and drove back the Morlocks and the shadows, I knelt down and lifted

her. The wood behind seemed full of the stir and murmur of a great company!

"She seemed to have fainted. I put her carefully
upon my shoulder and rose to push on, and then there
came a horrible realization. In manoeuvring with my
matches and Weena, I had turned myself about several
times, and now I had not the faintest idea in what
direction lay my path. For all I knew, I might be facing
back towards the Palace of Green Porcelain. I found
myself in a cold sweat. I had to think rapidly what to
do. I determined to build a fire and encamp where we
were. I put Weena, still motionless, down upon a turfy
hole, and very hastily, as my first lump of camphor
waned, I began collecting sticks and leaves. Here and
there out of the darkness round me the Morlocks' eyes
shone like carbuncles.

"The camphor flickered and went out. I lit a match,
and as I did so, two white forms that had been approaching Weena dashed hastily away. One was so
blinded by the light that he came straight for me, and
I felt his bones grind under the blow of my fist. He
gave a whoop of dismay, staggered a little way, and
fell down. I lit another piece of camphor, and went
on gathering my bonfire. Presently I noticed how dry
was some of the foliage above me, for since my arrival
on the Time Machine, a matter of a week, no rain had
fallen. So, instead of casting about among the trees for
fallen twigs, I began leaping up and dragging down
branches. Very soon I had a choking smoky fire of
green wood and dry sticks, and could economize my
camphor. Then I turned to where Weena lay beside
my iron mace. I tried what I could to revive her, but
she lay like one dead. I could not even satisfy myself
whether or not she breathed.

"Now, the smoke of the fire beat over towards me,

and it must have made me heavy of a sudden. More-over, the vapour of camphor was in the air. My fire would not need replenishing for an hour or so. I felt very weary after my exertion, and sat down. The wood, too, was full of a slumbrous murmur that I did not understand. I seemed just to nod and open my eyes. But all was dark, and the Morlocks had their hands upon me. Flinging off their clinging fingers I hastily felt in my pocket for the match-box, and—it had gone! Then they gripped and closed with me again. In a moment I knew what had happened. I had slept, and my fire had gone out, and the bitterness of death came over my soul. The forest seemed full of the smell of burning wood. I was caught by the neck, by the hair, by the arms, and pulled down. It was indescribably horrible in the darkness to feel all these soft creatures heaped upon me. I felt as if I was in a monstrous spider's web. I was overpowered, and went down. I felt little teeth nipping at my neck. I rolled over, and as I did so my hand came against my iron lever. It gave me strength. I struggled up, shaking the human rats from me, and, holding the bar short, I thrust where I judged their faces might be. I could feel the succulent giving of flesh and bone under my blows, and for a moment I was free.

"The strange exultation that so often seems to ac-company hard fighting came upon me. I knew that both I and Weena were lost, but I determined to make the Morlocks pay for their meat. I stood with my back to a tree, swinging the iron bar before me. The whole wood was full of the stir and cries of them. A minute passed. Their voices seemed to rise to a higher pitch of excitement, and their movements grew faster. Yet none came within reach. I stood glaring at the black-ness. Then suddenly came hope. What if the Morlocks were afraid? And close on the heels of that came a strange thing. The darkness seemed to grow luminous. Very dimly I began to see the Morlocks about me—three battered at my feet—and then I recognized, with incredulous surprise, that the others were running, in an incessant stream, as it seemed, from behind me, and away through the wood in front. And their backs seemed no longer white, but reddish. As I stood agape, I saw a little red spark go drifting across a gap of starlight between the branches, and vanish. And at that I understood the smell of burning wood, the slumbrous murmur that was growing now into a gusty roar, the red glow, and the Morlocks' flight.

"Stepping out from behind my tree and looking back, I saw, through the black pillars of the nearer trees, the flames of the burning forest. It was my first fire coming after me. With that I looked for Weena, but she was gone. The hissing and crackling behind me, the explosive thud as each fresh tree burst into flame, left little time for reflection. My iron bar still gripped, I followed in the Morlocks' path. It was a close race. Once the flames crept forward so swiftly on my right as I ran that I was outflanked and had to strike off to the left. But at last I emerged upon a small open space, and as I did so, a Morlock came blundering towards me, and past me, and went on straight into the fire!

"And now I was to see the most weird and horrible thing, I think, of all that I beheld in that future age. This whole space was as bright as day with the reflection of the fire. In the centre was a hillock or tumulus, surmounted by a scorched hawthorn. Beyond this was another arm of the burning forest, with yellow tongues already writhing from it, completely encircling the space with a fence of fire. Upon the hill-side were some thirty or forty Morlocks, dazzled by the light and heat, and blundering hither and thither against each other in their bewilderment. At first I did not realize their blindness, and struck furiously at them with my bar, in a frenzy of fear, as they approached me, killing one and crippling several more. But when I had watched the gestures of one of them groping under the hawthorn against the red sky, and heard their moans, I was assured of their absolute helplessness and misery in the glare, and I struck no more of them.

"Yet every now and then one would come straight towards me, setting loose a quivering horror that made me quick to elude him. At one time the flames died down somewhat, and I feared the foul creatures would presently be able to see me. I was thinking of beginning the fight by killing some of them before this should happen; but the fire burst out again brightly, and I stayed my hand. I walked about the hill among them and avoided them, looking for some trace of Weena. But Weena was gone.

"At last I sat down on the summit of the hillock, and watched this strange incredible company of blind things groping to and fro, and making uncanny noises to each other, as the glare of the fire beat on them. The coiling uprush of smoke streamed across the sky, and through the rare tatters of that red canopy, remote as though they belonged to another universe, shone the little stars. Two or three Morlocks came blundering into me, and I drove them off with blows of my fists, trembling as I did so.

"For the most part of that night I was persuaded it was a nightmare. I bit myself and screamed in a passionate desire to awake. I beat the ground with my hands, and got up and sat down again, and wandered here and there, and again sat down. Then I would fall to rubbing my eyes and calling upon God to let me awake. Thrice I saw Morlocks put their heads down in a kind of agony and rush into the flames. But, at last, above the subsiding red of the fire, above the streaming masses of black smoke and the whitening and blackening tree stumps, and the diminishing numbers of these dim creatures, came the white light of the day.

"I searched again for traces of Weena, but there were none. It was plain that they had left her poor little body in the forest. I cannot describe how it relieved me to think that it had escaped the awful fate to which it seemed destined. As I thought of that, I was almost moved to begin a massacre of the helpless abominations about me, but I contained myself. The hillock, as I have said, was a kind of island in the forest. From its summit I could now make out through a haze of smoke the Palace of Green Porcelain, and from that I could get my bearings for the White Sphinx. And so, leaving the remnant of these damned souls still going hither and thither and moaning, as the day grew clearer, I tied some grass about my feet and limped on across smoking ashes and among black stems, that still pulsated internally with fire, towards the hiding-place of the Time Machine. I walked slowly, for I was almost exhausted, as well as lame, and I felt the intensest wretchedness for the horrible death of little Weena. It seemed an overwhelming calamity. Now, in this old familiar room, it is more like the sorrow of a dream than an actual loss. But that morning it left me absolutely lonely again—terribly alone. I began to think of this house of mine, of this fireside, of some of you, and with such thoughts came a longing that was pain.

"But, as I walked over the smoking ashes under the bright morning sky, I made a discovery. In my trouser pocket were still some loose matches. The box must have leaked before it was lost.

10

"ABOUT EIGHT OR NINE in the morning I came to the same seat of yellow metal from which I had viewed the world upon the evening of my arrival. I thought of my hasty conclusions upon that evening and could not refrain from laughing bitterly at my confidence. Here was the same beautiful scene, the same abundant foliage, the same splendid palaces and magnificent ruins, the same silver river running between its fertile banks. The gay robes of the beautiful people moved hither and thither among the trees. Some were bathing in exactly the place where I had saved Weena, and that suddenly gave me a keen stab of pain. And like blots upon the landscape rose the cupolas above the ways to the Under-world. I understood now what all the beauty of the Over-world people covered. Very pleasant was their day, as pleasant as the day of the cattle in the field. Like the cattle, they knew of no enemies and provided against no needs. And their end was the same.

"I grieved to think how brief the dream of the human intellect had been. It had committed suicide. It had set itself steadfastly towards comfort and ease, a balanced society with security and permanency as its watchword, it had attained its hopes—to come to this at last. Once, life and property must have reached almost absolute safety. The rich had been assured of his wealth and comfort, the toiler assured of his life and work. No doubt in that perfect world there had been no unemployed problem, no social question left unsolved. And a great quiet had followed.

"It is a law of nature we overlook, that intellectual versatility is the compensation for change, danger, and trouble. An animal perfectly in harmony with its environment is a perfect mechanism. Nature never appeals to intelligence until habit and instinct are useless. There is no intelligence where there is no change and no need of change. Only those animals partake of intelligence that have to meet a huge variety of needs and dangers.

"So, as I see it, the Upper-world man had drifted towards his feeble prettiness, and the Under-world to mere mechanical industry. But that perfect state had lacked one thing even for mechanical perfection—absolute permanency. Apparently as time went on, the feeding of the Under-world, however it was effected, had become disjointed. Mother Necessity, who had been staved off for a few thousand years, came back again, and she began below. The Under-world being in contact with machinery, which, however perfect, still needs some little thought outside habit, had probably retained perforce rather more initiative, if less of every other human character, than the Upper. And when other meat failed them, they turned to what old habit had hitherto forbidden. So I say I saw it in my last view of the world of Eight Hundred and Two Thousand Seven Hundred and One. It may be as wrong an explanation as mortal wit could invent. It is how the thing shaped itself to me, and as that I give it to you.

"After the fatigues, excitements, and terrors of the past days, and in spite of my grief, this seat and the

tranquil view and the warm sunlight were very pleasant. I was very tired and sleepy, and soon my theoriz-
ing passed into dozing. Catching myself at that, I took
my own hint, and spreading myself out upon the turf
I had a long and refreshing sleep.

"I awoke a little before sunsetting. I now felt safe
against being caught napping by the Morlocks, and,
stretching myself, I came on down the hill towards the
White Sphinx. I had my crowbar in one hand, and the
other hand played with the matches in my pocket.

"And now came a most unexpected thing. As I approached the pedestal of the sphinx I found the
bronze valves were open. They had slid down into
grooves.

"At that I stopped short before them, hesitating
to enter.

"Within was a small apartment, and on a raised
place in the corner of this was the Time Machine. I
had the small levers in my pocket. So here, after all
my elaborate preparations for the siege of the White
Sphinx, was a meek surrender. I threw my iron bar
away, almost sorry not to use it.

"A sudden thought came into my head as I stooped
towards the portal. For once, at least, I grasped the
mental operations of the Morlocks. Suppressing a
strong inclination to laugh, I stepped through the
bronze frame and up to the Time Machine. I was surprised to find it had been carefully oiled and cleaned.
I have suspected since that the Morlocks had even
partially taken it to pieces while trying in their dim
way to grasp its purpose.

"Now as I stood and examined it, finding a pleasure
in the mere touch of the contrivance, the thing I had
expected happened. The bronze panels suddenly slid
up and struck the frame with a clang. I was in the

dark—trapped. So the Morlocks thought. At that I chuckled gleefully.

"I could already hear their murmuring laughter as they came towards me. Very calmly I tried to strike the match. I had only to fix on the levers and depart then like a ghost. But I had overlooked one little thing. The matches were of that abominable kind that light only on the box.

"You may imagine how all my calm vanished. The little brutes were close upon me. One touched me. I made a sweeping blow in the dark at them with the levers, and began to scramble into the saddle of the machine. Then came one hand upon me and then another. Then I had simply to fight against their persistent fingers for my levers, and at the same time feel for the studs over which these fitted. One, indeed, they almost got away from me. As it slipped from my hand, I had to butt in the dark with my head—I could hear the Morlock's skull ring—to recover it. It was a nearer thing than the fight in the forest, I think, this last scramble.

"But at last the lever was fixed and pulled over. The clinging hands slipped from me. The darkness presently fell from my eyes. I found myself in the same grey light and tumult I have already described.

11

"I HAVE already told you of the sickness and confusion that comes with time travelling. And this time I was not seated properly in the saddle, but sideways and in an unstable fashion. For an indefinite time I clung to the machine as it swayed and vibrated, quite unheeding how I went, and when I brought myself to look at the dials again I was amazed to find where I had arrived. One dial records days, and another thousands of days, another millions of days, and another thousands of millions. Now, instead of reversing the levers, I had pulled them over so as to go forward with them, and when I came to look at these indicators I found that the thousands hand was sweeping round as fast as the seconds hand of a watch—into futurity.

"As I drove on, a peculiar change crept over the appearance of things. The palpitating greyness grew darker; then—though I was still travelling with prodigious velocity—the blinking succession of day and night, which was usually indicative of a slower pace, returned, and grew more and more marked. This puzzled me very much at first. The alternations of night and day grew slower and slower, and so did the passage of the sun across the sky, until they seemed to stretch through centuries. At last a steady twilight brooded over the earth, a twilight only broken now and then when a comet glared across the darkling sky. The band of light that had indicated the sun had long since disappeared; for the sun had ceased to set—it simply rose and fell in the west, and grew ever broader and more red. All trace of the moon had vanished. The circling of the stars, growing slower and slower, had given place to creeping points of light. At last, some time before I stopped, the sun, red and very large, halted motionless upon the horizon, a vast dome glowing with a dull heat, and now and then suffering a momentary extinction. At one time it had for a little while glowed more brilliantly again, but it speedily reverted to its sullen red heat. I perceived by this slowing down of its rising and setting that the work of the tidal drag was done. The earth had come to rest with one face to the sun, even as in our own time the moon faces the earth. Very cautiously, for I remembered my former headlong fall, I began to reverse my motion. Slower and slower went the circling hands until the thousands one seemed motionless and the daily one was no longer a mere mist upon its scale. Still slower, until the dim outlines of a desolate beach grew visible.

"I stopped very gently and sat upon the Time Machine, looking round. The sky was no longer blue. North-eastward it was inky black, and out of the blackness shone brightly and steadily the pale white stars. Overhead it was a deep Indian red and starless, and south-eastward it grew brighter to a glowing scarlet where, cut by the horizon, lay the huge hull of the sun, red and motionless. The rocks about me were of a harsh reddish colour, and all the trace of life that I could see at first was the intensely green vegetation that covered every projecting point on their south-eastern face. It was the same rich green that one sees on forest moss or on the lichen in caves: plants which like these grow in a perpetual twilight.

"The machine was standing on a sloping beach. The sea stretched away to the south-west, to rise into a sharp bright horizon against the wan sky. There were no breakers and no waves, for not a breath of wind was stirring. Only a slight oily swell rose and fell like a gentle breathing, and showed that the eternal sea was still moving and living. And along the margin where the water sometimes broke was a thick incrustation of salt—pink under the lurid sky. There was a sense of oppression in my head, and I noticed that I was breathing very fast. The sensation reminded me of my only experience of mountaineering, and from that I judged the air to be more rarefied than it is now.

"Far away up the desolate slope I heard a harsh scream, and saw a thing like a huge white butterfly go slanting and fluttering up into the sky and, circling, disappear over some low hillocks beyond. The sound of its voice was so dismal that I shivered and seated myself more firmly upon the machine. Looking round me again, I saw that, quite near, what I had taken to be a reddish mass of rock was moving slowly towards me. Then I saw the thing was really a monstrous crab-like creature. Can you imagine a crab as large as yonder table, with its many legs moving slowly and uncertainly, its big claws swaying, its long antennae, like carters' whips, waving and feeling, and its stalked eyes gleaming at you on either side of its metallic front? Its back was corrugated and ornamented with ungainly bosses, and a greenish incrustation blotched it here and there. I could see the many palps of its complicated mouth flickering and feeling as it moved.

"As I stared at this sinister apparition crawling towards me, I felt a tickling on my cheek as though a fly had lighted there. I tried to brush it away with my hand, but in a moment it returned, and almost immediately came another by my ear. I struck at this, and caught something threadlike. It was drawn swiftly out of my hand. With a frightful qualm, I turned, and I saw that I had grasped the antenna of another monster crab that stood just behind me. Its evil eyes were wriggling on their stalks, its mouth was all alive with appetite, and its vast ungainly claws, smeared with an algal slime, were descending upon me. In a moment my hand was on the lever, and I had placed a month between myself and these monsters. But I was still on the same beach, and I saw them distinctly now as soon as I stopped. Dozens of them seemed to be crawling here and there, in the sombre light, among the foliated sheets of intense green.

"I cannot convey the sense of abominable desolation that hung over the world. The red eastern sky, the northward blackness, the salt Dead Sea, the stony beach crawling with these foul, slow-stirring monsters, the uniform poisonous-looking green of the lichenous plants, the thin air that hurts one's lungs: all contributed to an appalling effect. I moved on a hundred years, and there was the same red sun—a little larger, a little duller the same dying sea, the same chill air, and the same crowd of earthy crustacea creeping in and out among the green weed and the red rocks. And in the westward sky, I saw a curved pale line like a vast new moon.

"So I travelled, stopping ever and again, in great strides of a thousand years or more, drawn on by the mystery of the earth's fate, watching with a strange fascination the sun grow larger and duller in the westward sky, and the life of the old earth ebb away. At last, more than thirty million years hence, the huge red-hot dome of the sun had come to obscure nearly a tenth part of the darkling heavens. Then I stopped once more, for the crawling multitude of crabs had disappeared, and the red beach, save for its livid green

liverworts and lichens, seemed lifeless. And now it was
flecked with white. A bitter cold assailed me. Rare
white flakes ever and again came eddying down. To
the north-eastward, the glare of snow lay under the
starlight of the sable sky and I could see an undulating
crest of hillocks pinkish white. There were fringes of
ice along the sea margin, with drifting masses further
out; but the main expanse of that salt ocean, all bloody
under the eternal sunset, was still unfrozen.

"I looked about me to see if any traces of animal
life remained. A certain indefinable apprehension still
kept me in the saddle of the machine. But I saw nothing moving, in earth or sky or sea. The green slime
on the rocks alone testified that life was not extinct.
A shallow sandbank had appeared in the sea and the
water had receded from the beach. I fancied I saw
some black object flopping about upon this bank, but
it became motionless as I looked at it, and I judged
that my eye had been deceived, and that the black
object was merely a rock. The stars in the sky were
intensely bright and seemed to me to twinkle very
little.

"Suddenly I noticed that the circular westward outline of the sun had changed; that a concavity, a bay,
had appeared in the curve. I saw this grow larger. For
a minute perhaps I stared aghast at this blackness that
was creeping over the day, and then I realized that an
eclipse was beginning. Either the moon or the planet
Mercury was passing across the sun's disk. Naturally,
at first I took it to be the moon, but there is much to
incline me to believe that what I really saw was the
transit of an inner planet passing very near to the
earth.

"The darkness grew apace; a cold wind began to
blow in freshening gusts from the east, and the showering white flakes in the air increased in number. From

the edge of the sea came a ripple and whisper. Beyond these lifeless sounds the world was silent. Silent? It would be hard to convey the stillness of it. All the sounds of man, the bleating of sheep, the cries of birds, the hum of insects, the stir that makes the background of our lives—all that was over. As the darkness thickened, the eddying flakes grew more abundant, dancing before my eyes; and the cold of the air more intense. At last, one by one, swiftly, one after the other, the white peaks of the distant hills vanished into blackness. The breeze rose to a moaning wind. I saw the black central shadow of the eclipse sweeping towards me. In another moment the pale stars alone were visible. All else was rayless obscurity. The sky was absolutely black.

"A horror of this great darkness came on me. The cold, that smote to my marrow, and the pain I felt in breathing, overcame me. I shivered, and a deadly nausea seized me. Then like a red-hot bow in the sky appeared the edge of the sun. I got off the machine to recover myself. I felt giddy and incapable of facing the return journey. As I stood sick and confused I saw again the moving thing upon the shoal—there was no mistake now that it was a moving thing—against the red water of the sea. It was a round thing, the size of a football perhaps, or, it may be, bigger, and tentacles trailed down from it; it seemed black against the weltering blood-red water, and it was hopping fitfully about. Then I felt I was fainting. But a terrible dread of lying helpless in that remote and awful twilight sustained me while I clambered upon the saddle.

12

"So I CAME BACK. For a long time I must have been insensible upon the machine. The blinking succession of the days and nights was resumed, the sun got golden again, the sky blue. I breathed with greater freedom. The fluctuating contours of the land ebbed and flowed. The hands spun backward upon the dials. At last I saw again the dim shadows of houses, the evidences of decadent humanity. These, too, changed and passed, and others came. Presently, when the million dial was at zero, I slackened speed. I began to recognize our own petty and familiar architecture, the thousands hand ran back to the starting-point, the night and day flapped slower and slower. Then the old walls of the laboratory came round me. Very gently, now, I slowed the mechanism down.

"I saw one little thing that seemed odd to me. I think I have told you that when I set out, before my velocity became very high, Mrs. Watchett had walked across the room, travelling, as it seemed to me, like a rocket. As I returned, I passed again across that minute when she traversed the laboratory. But now her every motion appeared to be the exact inversion of her previous ones. The door at the lower end opened, and she glided quietly up the laboratory, back foremost, and disappeared behind the door by which she had previously entered. Just before that I seemed to see Hillyer for a moment; but he passed like a flash.

"Then I stopped the machine, and saw about me again the old familiar laboratory, my tools, my appliances just as I had left them. I got off the thing very shakily, and sat down upon my bench. For several minutes I trembled violently. Then I became calmer. Around me was my old workshop again, exactly as it had been. I might have slept there, and the whole thing have been a dream.

"And yet, not exactly! The thing had started from the south east corner of the laboratory. It had come to rest again in the north-west, against the wall where you saw it. That gives you the exact distance from my little lawn to the pedestal of the White Sphinx, into which the Morlocks had carried my machine.

"For a time my brain went stagnant. Presently I got up and came through the passage here, limping, because my heel was still painful, and feeling sorely begrimed. I saw the *Pall Mall Gazette* on the table by the door. I found the date was indeed to-day, and looking at the timepiece, saw the hour was almost eight o'clock. I heard your voices and the clatter of plates. I hesitated—I felt so sick and weak. Then I sniffed good wholesome meat, and opened the door on you. You know the rest. I washed, and dined, and now I am telling you the story.

"I know," he said, after a pause, "that all this will be absolutely incredible to you. To me the one incredible thing is that I am here to-night in this old familiar room looking into your friendly faces and telling you these strange adventures."

He looked at the Medical Man. "No. I cannot expect you to believe it. Take it as a lie—or a prophecy. Say I dreamed it in the workshop. Consider I have been speculating upon the destinies of our race

until I have hatched this fiction. Treat my assertion
of its truth as a mere stroke of art to enhance its
interest. And taking it as a story, what do you think
of it?"

He took up his pipe, and began, in his old accustomed manner, to tap with it nervously upon the bars
of the grate. There was a momentary stillness. Then
chairs began to creak and shoes to scrape upon the
carpet. I took my eyes off the Time Traveller's face,
and looked round at his audience. They were in the
dark, and little spots of colour swam before them. The
Medical Man seemed absorbed in the contemplation
of our host. The Editor was looking hard at the end
of his cigar—the sixth. The Journalist fumbled for his
watch. The others, as far as I remember, were motionless.

The Editor stood up with a sigh. "What a pity it is
you're not a writer of stories!" he said, putting his
hand on the Time Traveller's shoulder.

"You don't believe it?"

"Well——"

"I thought not."

The Time Traveller turned to us. "Where are the
matches?" he said. He lit one and spoke over his pipe,
puffing. "To tell you the truth . . . I hardly believe it
myself. . . . And yet . . ."

His eyes fell with a mute inquiry upon the withered
white flowers upon the little table. Then he turned
over the hand holding his pipe, and I saw he was
looking at some half-healed scars on his knuckles.

The Medical Man rose, came to the lamp, and examined the flowers. "The gynaeceum's odd," he said.
The Psychologist leant forward to see, holding out his
hand for a specimen.

"I'm hanged if it isn't a quarter to one," said the
Journalist. "How shall we get home?"

"Plenty of cabs at the station," said the Psychologist.

"It's a curious thing," said the Medical Man; "but I certainly don't know the natural order of these flowers. May I have them?"

The Time Traveller hesitated. Then suddenly: "Certainly not."

"Where did you really get them?" said the Medical Man.

The Time Traveller put his hand to his head. He spoke like one who was trying to keep hold of an idea that eluded him. "They were put into my pocket by Weena, when I travelled into Time." He stared round the room. "I'm damned if it isn't all going. This room and you and the atmosphere of every day is too much for my memory. Did I ever make a Time Machine, or a model of a Time Machine? Or is it all only a dream? They say life is a dream, a precious poor dream at times—but I can't stand another that won't fit. It's madness. And where did the dream come from? . . . I must look at that machine. If there *is* one!"

He caught up the lamp swiftly, and carried it, flaring red, through the door into the corridor. We followed him. There in the flickering light of the lamp was the machine sure enough, squat, ugly, and askew; a thing of brass, ebony, ivory, and translucent glimmering quartz. Solid to the touch—for I put out my hand and felt the rail of it—and with brown spots and smears upon the ivory, and bits of grass and moss upon the lower parts, and one rail bent awry.

The Time Traveller put the lamp down on the bench, and ran his hand along the damaged rail. "It's all right now," he said. "The story I told you was true. I'm sorry to have brought you out here in the cold." He took up the lamp, and, in an absolute silence, we returned to the smoking-room.

He came into the hall with us and helped the Editor on with his coat. The Medical Man looked into his face and, with a certain hesitation, told him he was suffering from overwork, at which he laughed hugely. I remember him standing in the open doorway, bawling good night.

I shared a cab with the Editor. He thought the tale a "gaudy lie." For my own part I was unable to come to a conclusion. The story was so fantastic and incredible, the telling so credible and sober. I lay awake most of the night thinking about it. I determined to go next day and see the Time Traveller again. I was told he was in the laboratory, and being on easy terms in the house, I went up to him. The laboratory, however, was empty. I stared for a minute at the Time Machine and put out my hand and touched the lever. At that the squat substantial-looking mass swayed like a bough shaken by the wind. Its instability startled me extremely, and I had a queer reminiscence of the childish days when I used to be forbidden to meddle. I came back through the corridor. The Time Traveller met me in the smoking-room. He was coming from the house. He had a small camera under one arm and a knapsack under the other. He laughed when he saw me, and gave me an elbow to shake. "I'm frightfully busy," said he, "with that thing in there."

"But is it not some hoax?" I said. "Do you really travel through time?"

"Really and truly I do." And he looked frankly into my eyes. He hesitated. His eyes wandered about the room. "I only want half an hour," he said. "I know why you came, and it's awfully good of you. There's some magazines here. If you'll stop to lunch I'll prove you this time travelling up to the hilt, specimen and all. If you'll forgive my leaving you now?"

I consented, hardly comprehending then the full import of his words, and he nodded and went on down the corridor. I heard the door of the laboratory slam, seated myself in a chair, and took up a daily paper. What was he going to do before lunch-time? Then suddenly I was reminded by an advertisement that I had promised to meet Richardson, the publisher, at two. I looked at my watch, and saw that I could barely save that engagement. I got up and went down the passage to tell the Time Traveller.

As I took hold of the handle of the door I heard an exclamation, oddly truncated at the end, and a click and a thud. A gust of air whirled round me as I opened the door, and from within came the sound of broken glass falling on the floor. The Time Traveller was not there. I seemed to see a ghostly, indistinct figure sitting in a whirling mass of black and brass for a moment—a figure so transparent that the bench behind with its sheets of drawings was absolutely distinct; but this phantasm vanished as I rubbed my eyes. The Time Machine had gone. Save for a subsiding stir of dust, the further end of the laboratory was empty. A pane of the skylight had, apparently, just been blown in.

I felt an unreasonable amazement. I knew that something strange had happened, and for the moment could not distinguish what the strange thing might be. As I stood staring, the door into the garden opened, and the man-servant appeared.

We looked at each other. Then ideas began to come. "Has Mr.——— gone out that way?" said I.

"No, sir. No one has come out this way. I was expecting to find him here."

At that I understood. At the risk of disappointing Richardson I stayed on, waiting for the Time Traveller; waiting for the second, perhaps still stranger story, and the specimens and photographs he would bring with him. But I am beginning now to fear that I must wait a lifetime. The Time Traveller vanished three years ago. And, as everybody knows now, he has never returned.

Epilogue

ONE CANNOT choose but wonder. Will he ever return? It may be that he swept back into the past, and
fell among the blood-drinking, hairy savages of the
Age of Unpolished Stone; into the abysses of the Cre-
taceous Sea; or among the grotesque saurians, the
huge reptilian brutes of the Jurassic times. He may
even now—if I may use the phrase—be wandering on
some plesiosaurus-haunted Oolitic coral reef, or beside the lonely saline lakes of the Triassic Age. Or did
he go forward, into one of the nearer ages, in which
men are still men, but with the riddles of our own
time answered and its wearisome problems solved?
Into the manhood of the race: for I, for my own part,
cannot think that these latter days of weak experiment, fragmentary theory, and mutual discord are indeed man's culminating time! I say, for my own part.
He, I know—for the question had been discussed
among us long before the Time Machine was made—
thought but cheerlessly of the Advancement of Mankind, and saw in the growing pile of civilization only
a foolish heaping that must inevitably fall back upon
and destroy its makers in the end. If that is so, it
remains for us to live as though it were not so. But
to me the future is still black and blank—is a vast
ignorance, lit at a few casual places by the memory of

his story. And I have by me, for my comfort, two strange white flowers—shrivelled now, and brown and flat and brittle—to witness that even when mind and strength had gone, gratitude and a mutual tenderness still lived on in the heart of man.

Appendix

Wells apparently edited this chapter (Chapter 11 in this Signet Classic edition) for the first book publication of *The Time Machine*. He maintained his cuts in the version published in the Atlantic Edition of his collected works, considered the standard and authoritative text. Nevertheless, there is sufficient interest in the Time Traveller's adventures to include this longer, more detailed version as an appendix.

Wells goes into fascinating detail about the future evolution of the human race. We will not read anything on human evolution more radical until Olaf Stapledon's *Last and First Men*, published in 1930.

—Greg Bear

14

The Further Vision

''I HAVE ALREADY told you of the sickness and confusion that comes with time travelling. And this time I was not seated properly in the saddle, but sideways and in an unstable fashion. For an indefinite time I clung to the machine as it swayed and vibrated, quite unheeding how I went, and when I brought myself to look at the dials again I was amazed to find where I had arrived. One dial records days, another thousands of days, another millions of days, and another thousands of millions. Now, instead of reversing the levers I had pulled them over so as to go forward with them, and when I came to look at these indicators I found that the thousands hand was sweeping round as fast as the seconds hands of a watch—into futurity. Very cautiously, for I remembered my former headlong fall, I began to reverse my motion. Slower and slower went the circling hands until the thousands one seemed motionless and the daily one was no longer a mere mist upon its scale. Still slower, until the grey haze around me became distincter and dim outlines of an undulating waste grew visible.

"I stopped. I was on a bleak moorland, covered with a sparse vegetation, and grey with a thin hoarfrost. The time was midday, the orange sun, shorn of its effulgence, brooded near the meridian in a sky of drabby grey. Only a few black bushes broke the monotony of the scene. The great buildings of the decadent men among whom, it seemed to me, I had been so recently, had vanished and left no trace: not a mound even marked their position. Hill and valley, sea and river—all, under the wear and work of the rain and frost, had melted into new forms. No doubt, too, the rain and snow had long since washed out the Morlock tunnels. A nipping breeze stung my hands and face. So far as I could see there were neither hills, nor trees, nor rivers: only an uneven stretch of cheerless plateau.

"Then suddenly a dark bulk rose out of the moor,

something that gleamed like a serrated row of iron plates, and vanished almost immediately in a depression. And then I became aware of a number of faint grey things, coloured to almost the exact tint of the frost-bitten soil, which were browsing here and there upon its scanty grass, and running to and fro. I saw one jump with a sudden start, and then my eye detected perhaps a score of them. At first I thought they were rabbits, or some small breed of kangaroo. Then, as one came hopping near me, I perceived that it belonged to neither of these groups. It was plantigrade, its hind legs rather the longer; it was tailless, and covered with a straight greyish hair that thickened about the head into a Skye terrier's mane. As I had understood that in the Golden Age man had killed out almost all the other animals, sparing only a few of the more ornamental, I was naturally curious about the creatures. They did not seem afraid of me, but browsed on, much as rabbits would do in a place unfrequented by men; and it occurred to me that I might perhaps secure a specimen.

"I got off the machine, and picked up a big stone. I had scarcely done so when one of the little creatures came within easy range. I was so lucky as to hit it on the head, and it rolled over at once and lay motionless. I ran to it at once. It remained still, almost as if it were killed. I was surprised to see that the thing had five feeble digits to both its fore and hind feet—the fore feet, indeed, were almost as human as the fore feet of a frog. It had, moreover, a roundish head, with a projecting forehead and forward-looking eyes, obscured by its lank hair. A disagreeable apprehension flashed across my mind. As I knelt down and seized my capture, intending to examine its teeth and other anatomical points which might show human characteristics, the metallic-looking object, to which I have already alluded, reappeared above a ridge in the moor, coming towards me and making a strange clattering sound as it came. Forthwith the grey animals about me began to answer with a short, weak yelping as if of terror—and bolted off in a direction opposite to that from which this new creature approached. They must have hidden in burrows or behind bushes and tussocks, for in a moment not one of them was visible.

"I rose to my feet, and stared at this grotesque monster. I can only describe it by comparing it to a centipede. It stood about three feet high, and had a long segmented body, perhaps thirty feet long, with curiously overlapping greenish-black plates. It seemed to crawl upon a multitude of feet, looping its body as it advanced. Its blunt round head, with a polygonal arrangement of black eye spots, carried two flexible, writhing, horn-like antenna. It was coming along, I should judge, at a pace of about eight or ten miles an hour, and it left me little time for thinking. Leaving my grey animal, or grey man, whichever it was, on the ground, I set off for the machine. Halfway I paused, regretting that abandonment, but a glance over my shoulder destroyed any such regret. When I gained the machine the monster was scarce fifty yards away. It was certainly not a vertebrated animal. It had no snout, and its mouth was fringed with jointed dark-coloured plates. But I did not care for a nearer view.

"I traversed one day and stopped again, hoping to find the colossus gone and some vestige of my victim; but, I should judge, the giant centipede did not trouble itself about bones. At any rate both had vanished. The faintly human touch of these little creatures perplexed me greatly. If you come to think, there is no reason why a degenerate humanity should not come at last to differentiate into as many species as the descendants of the mud fish who fathered all the land vertebrates. I saw no more of any insect colossus, as to my thinking the segmented creature must have been. Evidently the physiological difficulty that at present keeps all the insects small had been surmounted at last, and this division of the animal kingdom had arrived at the long-awaited supremacy which its enormous energy and vitality deserve. I made several attempts to kill or capture another of the greyish vermin, but none of my missiles were so successful as my first; and, after perhaps a dozen disappointing throws, that left my arm aching, I felt a gust of irritation at my folly in coming so far into futurity without weapons or equipment. I resolved to run on for one glimpse of the still remoter future—one peep into the deeper abysm of time—and then to return to you and my own epoch. Once more I remounted the machine, and once more the world grew hazy and grey.

"As I drove on, a peculiar change crept over the appearance of things. The palpitating greyness grew darker; then—though I was still travelling with prodigious velocity—the blinking succession of day and night, which was usually indicative of a slower pace, returned, and grew more and more marked. This puzzled me very much at first. The alternations of night and day grew slower and slower, and so did the passage of the sun across the sky, until they seemed to stretch through centuries. At last a steady twilight brooded over the earth, a twilight only broken now and then when a comet glared across the darkling sky. The band of light that had indicated the sun had long since disappeared; for the sun had ceased to set—it simply rose and fell in the west, and grew ever broader and more red. All trace of the moon had vanished. The circling of the stars, growing slower and slower, had given place to creeping points of light. At last, some time before I stopped, the sun, red and very large, halted motionless upon the horizon, a vast dome glowing with a dull heat, and now and then suffering a momentary extinction. At one time it had for a little while glowed more brilliantly again, but it speedily reverted to its sullen red-heat. I perceived by this slowing down of its rising and setting that the work of the tidal drag was done. The earth had come to rest with one face to the sun, even as in our own time the moon faces the earth. Very cautiously, for I remembered my former headlong fall, I began to reverse my motion. Slower and slower went the circling hands until the thousands one seemed motionless, and the daily one was no longer a mere mist upon its scale. Still slower, until the dim outlines of a desolate beach grew visible.

"I stopped very gently and sat upon the Time Machine, looking round. The sky was no longer blue. North-eastward it was inky black, and out of the blackness shone brightly and steadily the pale white stars. Overhead it was a deep Indian red and starless, and south-eastward it grew brighter to a glowing scarlet where, cut by the horizon, lay the huge hull of the sun, red and motionless. The rocks about me were of a harsh reddish colour, and all the trace of life that I could see at first was the intensely green vegetation that covered every projecting point on their south-eastern face. It was the same rich green that one sees on forest moss or on the lichen in caves: plants which like these grow in a perpetual twilight.

"The machine was standing on a sloping beach. The sea stretched away to the south-west, to rise into a sharp bright horizon against the wan sky. There were no breakers and no waves, for not a breath of wind was stirring. Only a slight oily swell rose and fell like a gentle breathing, and showed that the eternal sea was still moving and living. And along the margin

where the water sometimes broke was a thick incrustation of salt-pink under the lurid sky. There was a sense
of oppression in my head, and I noticed that I was
breathing very fast. The sensation reminded me of my
only experience of mountaineering, and from that I
judged the air to be more rarefied than it is now.

"Far away up the desolate slope I heard a harsh
scream, and saw a thing like a huge white butterfly go
slanting and fluttering up into the sky and, circling,
disappear over some low hillocks beyond. The sound
of its voice was so dismal that I shivered and seated
myself more firmly upon the machine. Looking round
me again, I saw that, quite near, what I had taken to
be a reddish mass of rock was moving slowly towards
me. Then I saw the thing was really a monstrous crab-
like creature. Can you imagine a crab as large as yonder table, with its many legs moving slowly and uncertainly, its big claws swaying, its long antenna, like
carters' whips, waving and feeling, and its stalked eyes
gleaming at you on either side of its metallic front?
Its back was corrugated and ornamented with ungainly
bosses, and a greenish incrustation blotched it here
and there. I could see the many palps of its complicated mouth flickering and feeling as it moved.

"As I stared at this sinister apparition crawling towards me, I felt a tickling on my cheek as though a
fly had lighted there. I tried to brush it away with
my hand, but in a moment it returned, and almost
immediately came another by my ear. I struck at this,
and caught something threadlike. It was drawn swiftly
out of my hand. With a frightful qualm, I turned, and
saw that I had grasped the antenna of another monster
crab that stood just behind me. Its evil eyes were wriggling on their stalks, its mouth was all alive with appetite, and its vast ungainly claws, smeared with an algal
slime, were descending upon me. In a moment my

hand was on the lever, and I had placed a month between myself and these monsters. But I was still on the same beach, and I saw them distinctly now as soon as I stopped. Dozens of them seemed to be crawling here and there, in the sombre light, among the foliated sheets of intense green.

"I cannot convey the sense of abominable desolation that hung over the world. The red eastern sky, the northward blackness, the salt Dead Sea, the stony beach crawling with these foul, slow-stirring monsters, the uniform poisonous-looking green of the lichenous plants, the thin air that hurts one's lungs: all contributed to an appalling effect. I moved on a hundred years, and there was the same red sun—a little larger, a little duller—the same dying sea, the same chill air, and the same crowd of earthy crustacea creeping in and out among the green weed and the red rocks. And in the westward sky I saw a curved pale line like a vast new moon.

"So I travelled, stopping ever and again, in great strides of a thousand years or more, drawn on by the mystery of the earth's fate, watching with a strange fascination the sun grow larger and duller in the westward sky, and the life of the old earth ebb away. At last, more than thirty million years hence, the huge red-hot dome of the sun had come to obscure nearly a tenth part of the darkling heavens. Then I stopped once more, for the crawling multitude of crabs had disappeared, and the red beach, save for its livid green liverworts and lichens, seemed lifeless. And now it was flecked with white. A bitter cold assailed me. Rare white flakes ever and again came eddying down. To the north-eastward, the glare of snow lay under the starlight of the sable sky, and I could see an undulating crest of hillocks pinkish-white. There were fringes of ice along the sea margin, with drifting masses further out; but the main expanse of that salt ocean, all bloody under the eternal sunset, was still unfrozen.

"I looked about me to see if any traces of animal-life remained. A certain indefinable apprehension still kept me in the saddle of the machine. But I saw nothing moving, in earth or sky or sea. The green slime on the rocks alone testified that life was not extinct. A shallow sandbank had appeared in the sea and the water had receded from the beach. I fancied I saw some black object flopping about upon this bank, but it became motionless as I looked at it, and I judged that my eye had been deceived, and that the black object was merely a rock. The stars in the sky were intensely bright and seemed to me to twinkle very little.

"Suddenly I noticed that the circular westward outline of the sun had changed; that a concavity, a bay, had appeared in the curve. I saw this grow larger. For a minute perhaps I stared aghast at this blackness that was creeping over the day, and then I realized that an eclipse was beginning. Either the moon or the planet Mercury was passing across the sun's disk. Naturally, at first I took it to be the moon, but there is much to incline me to believe that what I really saw was the transit of an inner planet passing very near to the earth.

"The darkness grew apace; a cold wind began to blow in freshening gusts from the east, and the showering white flakes in the air increased in number. From the edge of the sea came a ripple and whisper. Beyond these lifeless sounds the world was silent. Silent? It would be hard to convey the stillness of it. All the sounds of man, the bleating of sheep, the cries of birds, the hum of insects, the stir that makes the background of our lives—all that was over. As the darkness thickened, the eddying flakes grew more abundant, dancing before my eyes; and the cold of the air more intense. At last, one by one, swiftly, one after the other, the white peaks of the distant hills vanished into blackness. The breeze rose to a moaning wind. I saw the black central shadow of the eclipse sweeping towards me. In another moment the pale stars alone were visible. All else was rayless obscurity. The sky was absolutely black.

"A horror of this great darkness came on me. The cold, that smote to my marrow, and the pain I felt in breathing overcame me. I shivered, and a deadly nausea seized me. Then like a red-hot bow in the sky appeared the edge of the sun. I got off the machine to recover myself. I felt giddy and incapable of facing the return journey. As I stood sick and confused I saw again the moving thing upon the shoal—there was no mistake now that it was a moving thing—against the red water of the sea. It was a round thing, the size of a football perhaps, or, it may be, bigger, and tentacles trailed down from it; it seemed black against the weltering blood-red water, and it was hopping fitfully about. Then I felt I was fainting. But a terrible dread of lying helpless in that remote and awful twilight sustained me while I clambered upon the saddle.

Afterword

To be able to travel in time is an understandably common human fantasy—to anticipate our own futures, to revisit and perhaps alter past lives—or to travel even further, to witness historical periods far beyond the spans of our own existences. Though we do not have the actual ability to time travel, narrative is itself a kind of technology that compensates for that lack. Storytelling is not subject to the even flow of chronological time in which we actually live but can proceed at its own pace, speeding up or slowing down, and even interrupt itself, jumping around in time through the use of prolepsis (flash forward) or analepsis (flashback). Narratives about time travel have still greater freedom in the ways that they make their journey from beginning to end.

Appropriately enough, H. G. Wells explicitly frames the act of storytelling within his seminal, brilliant "scientific romance" *The Time Machine:* "Story!" cries the Editor when the Time Traveller returns from his journey to the future (page 16). The main section of the book features the hero recounting his story to his friends as they sit around his dinner table on extra-comfortable chairs of his own invention. In doing so, he is traveling both forward and backward in time, recalling from memory his experiences in the future. The story-within-a-story is a common device in the supernatural tale for addressing the issues of plausibility raised by writing in a genre outside of conventional realism—as if such a story knows itself to be a story. Think, for instance, of Henry James's both playful and traumatic ghost story *The Turn of the Screw*. Wells wrote later in his *Experiment in Autobiography*, "I had realised that the more impossible the story I had to tell, the more ordinary must be the setting, and the circumstances in which I now set the Time Traveller were all that I could imagine of solid, upper-middle-class comfort."

What makes a story fantastic, or science fiction, is its contradicting something that is generally believed to be the case. This is just how the Time Traveller begins his story at the book's first dinner party: "I shall have to controvert one or two ideas that are almost universally accepted. The geometry, for instance, they taught you at school is founded on a misconception" (page 1). Adopting a controversial position in an effort to educate his audience was a strategy that became characteristic of Wells himself. By the publication of *The Time Machine*, following a health scare, he had abandoned teaching for writing and was already the author of the scientific textbooks *A Textbook of Biology* and *Honours Physiography*. He claimed in his later book of essays, *Mankind in the Making,* that "scolding the schoolmaster [. . .] is an amusement so entirely congenial to my temperament that I do not for one moment propose to abandon it." His eventual output of more than one hundred fifty books and pamphlets comprised both nonfiction writing and fiction that sought to improve the world through strong educational messages; many of these messages ran against the current of commonly held beliefs, such as on the origin of mankind, the sanctity of marriage, or the desirability of the nation-state.

The Time Traveller's first lesson is that in order for an object to exist it must have four dimensions, as proven by the power of his time machine to travel in this fourth dimension as easily as mobile organisms are able to travel in the other three. *The Time Machine* was not the first time-travel narrative, of course, but it was more usual for characters to time-travel the same way humans naturally remove themselves from the experience of time passing: sleep, as in William Morris's *News from*

Nowhere, which *The Time Machine* parodies, or Wells's own later *When the Sleeper Wakes*. Wells's innovation within the time-travel story is suggested by the title of his book (in manuscript it was called "The Time Traveller"), and by its original subtitle *An Invention*. The Time Traveller is able to experience 802,701 and other years besides—in the *New Review* version, he experiences a further vision of creatures that resemble a kangaroo and a centipede, while in the manuscript he visits the seventeenth century—because of the quality of his technology. The Time Machine is the product both of his own individual, entrepreneurial innovation, and, ultimately, of the historical forces of the Industrial Revolution.

Throughout his career, Wells was obsessed with technology, and in particular technologies of transport. Karl Marx is reputed to have hailed the invention of the railways as the "annihilation of space by time"; Wells's first political-futurological work, *Anticipations*, speculates on the "abolition of distances" by modern technologies. Later works imagine vehicles such as the Martian spacecraft and tripods of *The War of the Worlds*, moving roadways in *When the Sleeper Wakes*, and the massive airships of *The War in the Air*. George Ponderevo's invention of powered flight in *Tono-Bungay* foreshadows that of the Wright Brothers by several years; Wells also imagines military technology, such as the tanks in his short story "The Land Ironclads" and aerial bombardment in the film *Things to Come*. Given the "abolition of distances" by such transformative technologies, he argues, it has become more important for neighbors newly rendered closer to get along with one another better. The catastrophic outcomes of these fantastic stories show the appalling consequences of different classes, species, and nations failing to do so: thus do these books seek to educate as well.

The Time Machine's range of travel exceeds even that of these devices, but Wells's ingeniously partial description of the machine's physical details suggests a resemblance to a much humbler but no less Victorian technology of transport. The machine's components include brass rails, nickel bars, and a quartz rod. When first learning how to steer it, the Time Traveller feels the machine sway beneath him and notes that, when mounted properly, one should not sit sideways, but astride. When arriving in the future, the Time Traveller falls off: clearly he has reenacted the experience of many Victorians and, in learning to use this new mode of transport, fallen off his bicycle.

Wells was himself an enthusiastic cyclist, and his later stories *The Wheels of Chance* and *The History of Mr. Polly* show the increased freedoms granted to their heroes by their ability to get around on this cheap, mass-produced transport. However, neither Hoopdriver nor Polly is able to travel very far up the social ladder, because of their humble class origins, relative poverty, and poor education. In contrast, The Time Traveller, judging by the affluent, champagne-drinking, "solid upper-middle-class" masculine clique of the Medical Man and the Provincial Mayor in which he is first seen, and also by his apparent lack of a job, would appear to have a private income, and thus the financial and technological resources to soup up his machine sufficiently to power him far beyond the historical environment of late-Victorian Britain.

Just, however, as Wells counseled against "excelsior" biology in science—the belief that humanity would continue evolving to ever further heights of intelligence, complexity, and beauty—so too does he warn here against the assumption that late-Victorian society would forever continue to be a rich and highly developed, superior society. Of this notion, the Time Traveller is very soon disabused.

Of the many shocks that await him in the future, the first is that the London he has left behind may already represent the peak of humanity's social and biological development, and that the future will see only decline. (For all of the enormous length of the Time Traveller's journey in time, it should be noted that he does not go very far at all in space—merely from one side of his laboratory to the other, raising the possibility that the world beyond southwest London has evolved into the technological utopia that he expects!) He explains to his audience of friends, "I had always anticipated that the people of the year Eight Hundred and Two Thousand odd would be incredibly in front of us in knowledge, art, everything. Then one of them suddenly asked me a question that showed him to be on the intellectual level of one of our five-year-old children" (page 27).

Intriguingly, this situation seems to have come about from an excess of comfort. At some stage in human history, the "haves" became too contented with their lot and ceased to struggle: not having been kept keen on the grindstones of either natural or sexual selection (the Eloi are constantly "making love in a half-playful fashion" [page 48]), the "human intellect [. . .] had committed suicide" (page 90). Half of humanity has become the pretty but foolish and childish Eloi. The Palace of Green Porcelain is not only a museum of human culture, it is all that remains of human culture. Wells was gleefully fond of using images of empty buildings to represent human or artistic productions that had lost their purpose. In 802,701, writing and abstract nouns have disappeared from language, and:

> All the traditions, the complex organizations, the nations, languages, literatures, aspirations, even the mere memory of Man as I knew him, had been swept out of existence. Instead were these frail creatures who had forgotten their high ancestry, and the white Things of which I went in terror.   (page 71)

Only technology has endured, maintained for the nefarious designs of the other half of human posterity, the cannibalistic and monstrous Morlocks, whose consumption of the descendants of the elite is a gruesome act of class revenge.

Not only must the Time Traveller revise his overoptimistic view of the future, but also of himself. (Wells's creations Doctor Moreau, the Martians, and the Invisible Man will also learn how apparent technological superiority fails to confer invulnerability.) For all of his brilliance in the present day as an inventor, the Time Traveller, he must himself admit, makes a poor show as a hero of Imperial Britain.

> I have thought since how particularly ill-equipped I was for such an experience. [. . .] I had come without arms, without medicine, without anything to smoke—at times I missed tobacco frightfully—even without enough matches. If only I had thought of a Kodak! I could have flashed that glimpse of the Under-world in a second, and examined it at leisure. But, as it was, I stood there with only the weapons and the powers that Nature had endowed me with—hands, feet, and teeth; these, and four safety-matches that still remained to me.
>
> (page 63)

Even as a simple, firsthand reader of the world of the future, the Time Traveller makes repeated failures of understanding. His telling of his own story is punctuated with self-interruptions such as: "This, I must remind you, was my speculation at the time. Later, I was to appreciate how far it fell short of the reality" (page 33), or "it was an obvious conclusion, but it was absolutely wrong" (page 46). On first arriving in 802,701, the Time Traveller is confronted by a white statue of a sphinx, the famously inscrutable mythical beast. In order to compensate for his lack of a nineteenth-century adventuring toolkit, the Time Traveller must decivilize himself into a brutally effective primitive man, temporarily eschewing all technology except in its most basic forms: the club and the means of making fire. Then he must turn himself into a solver of ancient riddles like Oedipus, who also walked with a limp and consulted the Sphinx in his adventure. The Sphinx asks "What walks on four legs in the morning, two legs in the afternoon, and three legs in the evening?" and the Time Traveller acts out in turn the answers: crawling baby (when he falls off his time machine), adult (when he stands up), and cane-bearing old man (when he secures his mace from the Palace of Green Porcelain).

"Man," in the sense of humankind, is also the answer to the riddle of the future, as the Time Traveller discovers first that the Eloi, then the Morlocks, are "heir to all the ages" (page 54), descendants of the fellow humans he has left behind. Such monstrous degeneration could be seen as the result of the Time Traveller's own confident and easy belief in the certainty of progress, or even humanity's unwillingness to heed the lessons of seers such as Wells and Thomas Carlyle, whose spirit the Time Traveller invokes. Perhaps the most positive reading of *The Time Machine* would be to take it as a warning, as an intervention: if humanity does not tackle economic inequality and poor education, then this future will be the result—but it is not too late for other futures yet. Indeed, in Stephen Baxter's authorized sequel, *The Time Ships*, the Time Traveller's telling of his story alters the nature of the future so that when he returns to 802,701, the future is different. For progress, both cultural and biological, to succeed, it must be managed, willed, driven, organized; otherwise awaits "the fate of energy in security; it takes to art and to eroticism, and then come languor and decay" (page 37).

Still worse visions await the Time Traveller as he escapes the Morlocks and voyages into the far, far future. Wells's imagination was powerfully attracted to scenes of destruction—often because the potential ruin of civilization can function as a pretext for the reconstruction of a better one. Here, however, as the Time Traveller stands upon mankind's "terminal beach," Wells's prose achieves a decadent, desolate beauty to which there can be no human answers:

> The darkness grew apace; a cold wind began to blow in freshening gusts from the east, and the showering white flakes in the air increased in number. From the edge of the sea came a ripple and whisper. Beyond these lifeless sounds the world was silent. Silent? It would be hard to convey the stillness of it. All the sounds of man, the bleating of

sheep, the cries of birds, the hum of insects, the stir that makes the background of our lives—all that was over. As the darkness thickened, the eddying flakes grew more abundant, dancing before my eyes; and the cold of the air more intense. At last, one by one, swiftly, one after the other, the white peaks of the distant hills vanished into blackness. The breeze rose to a moaning wind. I saw the black central shadow of the eclipse sweeping towards me. In another moment the pale stars alone were visible. All else was rayless obscurity. The sky was absolutely black. (pages 98–99)

The Time Machine is permeated with images of light and dark. Wells was very fond of the metaphor, which goes back at least to the Ancient Greeks, of light for knowledge and darkness for ignorance: in his essay "The Rediscovery of the Unique," he declares that "science is a match that man has just got alight." Fire, the most basic Promethean technology, might be developed into more complex and sophisticated forms or, as here, might go out. This eclipse is a prefiguring of the death of our sun and of all life on Earth, even the very basic posthuman life-forms he sees on the beach, the "sunset of mankind" that the Time Traveller has already witnessed (page 34).

The hero wearily delivers news of this forthcoming apocalypse to an audience that remains skeptical and unbelieving. Who, after all, can blame them? The storyteller, "one of those men who are too clever to be believed" (page 12), is asking his audience to accept a great deal, resignedly inviting them to "take it as a lie—or a prophecy. Say I dreamed it in the workshop. Consider I have been speculating upon the destinies of our race until I have hatched this fiction" (pages 101–2). For each of the story's tellers, narrative told in ordinary human language is a technology insufficient to convey the reality of actually traveling in time:

In writing it down I feel with only too much keenness the inadequacy of pen and ink—and, above

all, my own inadequacy—to express its quality.
You read, I will suppose, attentively enough; but
you cannot see the speaker's white, sincere face in
the bright circle of the little lamp, nor hear the intonation of his voice. You cannot know how his
expression followed the turns of his story! Most of
us hearers were in shadow, for the candles in the
smoking-room had not been lighted, and only the
face of the Journalist and the legs of the Silent
Man from the knees downward were illuminated.
At first we glanced now and again at each other.
After a time we ceased to do that, and looked only
at the Time Traveller's face.   (page 18)

The setting for the Time Traveller's narration is
strongly reminiscent of a scene of hypnosis or sleight of
hand, a conjuring trick. However, perhaps the proof of
the Time Traveller's story is his own ultimate absence
from it. If he wanted to cover his own disappearance,
why concoct such an elaborate story as this? More likely
for him, surely, would be one of the grisly fates at the
hands of cavemen or claws of dinosaurs that the frame
narrator imagines. The outer narrative closes in thinking
of Weena, the child-woman whose life the Time Traveller saves, and whose death he also inadvertently causes,
but who emerges as the book's unlikely symbol of hope.
The Time Traveller himself, we are told:

. . . thought but cheerlessly of the Advancement of
Mankind, and saw in the growing pile of civilization only a foolish heaping that must inevitably fall
back upon and destroy its makers in the end. If that
is so, it remains for us to live as though it were not
so. But to me the future is still black and blank—is
a vast ignorance, lit at a few casual places by the
memory of his story.   (pages 107–8)

The flowers brought back from the future do not belong
to any "natural order" known to the Medical Man (page
103), and might be material proof of the Time Traveller's

journey in time, but also proof that "even when mind and strength had gone, gratitude and a mutual tenderness still lived on in the heart of man" (page 108). For all of the awe and terror induced by Wells's possible vision of the future, such acts of affection, of bonding, offer the possibility that indeed the Time Traveller's vision may not be so. An attentive reader or listener of this fantastic story of things that are not so—or, at least, are not so yet—is invited not just to consume, but to learn from it. If the future is indeed "still black and blank," then it can still be illuminated by the narratives that might yet be imagined there.

—Simon J. James

Selected Bibliography

Books by H. G. Wells

The Time Machine: An Invention (1895) novel
The Stolen Bacillus and Other Incidents (1895) short stories
The Wonderful Visit (1895) novel
The Island of Dr. Moreau: A Possibility (1896) novel
The Wheels of Chance: A Holiday Adventure Novel (1896) novel
The Plattner Story, and Others (1897) short stories
The Invisible Man: A Grotesque Romance (1897) novel
Thirty Strange Stories (1897) short stories
The War of the Worlds (1898) novel
When the Sleeper Wakes: A Story of the Years to Come (1899) novel
Tales of Space and Time (1899) short stories
Love and Mr. Lewisham: The Story of a Very Young Couple (1900) novel
Anticipations of the Reaction of Mechanical and Scientific Progress upon Human Life and Thought (1901) nonfiction
The First Men in the Moon (1901) novel
The Sea Lady: A Tissue of Moonshine (1902) novel
Mankind in the Making (1903) nonfiction
Twelve Stories and a Dream (1903) short stories
The Food of the Gods, and How It Came to Earth (1904) novel
A Modern Utopia (1905) novel
Kipps: The Story of a Simple Soul (1905) novel

In the Days of the Comet (1906) novel

First and Last Things: A Confession of Faith and a Rule of Life (1908) nonfiction

The War in the Air, and Particularly How Mr. Bert Smallways Fared While It Lasted (1908) novel

Tono-Bungay (1908) novel

Ann Veronica: A Modern Love Story (1909) novel

New Worlds for Old (1909) nonfiction

The History of Mr. Polly (1910) novel

The Country of the Blind, and Other Stories (1911) short stories

The Door in the Wall, and Other Stories (1911) short stories

The New Machiavelli (1911) novel

Marriage (1912) novel

The Passionate Friends: A Novel (1913) novel

The World Set Free: A Story of Mankind (1914) novel

The War That Will End War (1914) nonfiction

The Wife of Sir Isaac Harman (1914) novel

Bealby: A Holiday (1915) novel

Boon, The Mind of the Race, The Wild Asses of the Devil, and The Last Trump: Being a First Selection from the Literary Remains of George Boon, Appropriate to the Times, Prepared for Publication by Reginald Bliss with an Ambiguous Introduction by H. G. Wells (1915) novel, as Reginald Bliss

The Research Magnificent (1915) novel

Mr. Britling Sees It Through (1916) novel

God, The Invisible King (1917) nonfiction

The Soul of a Bishop: A Novel (with Just a Little Love in It) About Conscience and Religion and the Real Troubles of Life (1917) novel

Joan and Peter: The Story of an Education (1918) novel

The Undying Fire: A Contemporary Novel (1919) novel

The Outline of History: Being a Plain History of Life and Mankind (1920) nonfiction

Russia in the Shadows (1920) nonfiction

The Salvaging of Civilisation: The Probable Future of Mankind (1921) nonfiction

The Secret Places of the Heart (1922) novel

Men Like Gods: A Novel (1923) novel

The Story of a Great Schoolmaster: Being a Plain Account of the Life and Ideas of Sanderson of Oundle (1924) nonfiction

The Dream: A Novel (1924) novel

Christina Alberta's Father (1925) novel

The World of William Clissold: A Novel at a New Angle (1926) novel

Meanwhile: A Picture of a Lady (1927) novel

Mr. Blettsworthy on Rampole Island (1928) novel

The Open Conspiracy: Blue Prints for a World Revolution (1928) nonfiction

The King Who Was a King: The Book of a Film (1929) novel

The Autocracy of Mr. Parham: His Remarkable Adventures in This Changing World (1930) novel

The Science of Life: A Summary of Contemporary Knowledge About Life and Its Possibilities (1931) nonfiction, with Julian Huxley and G. P. Wells

The Work, Wealth and Happiness of Mankind (1931) nonfiction

The Bulpington of Blup: Adventures, Poses, Stresses, Conflicts, and Disaster in a Contemporary Brain (1932) novel

The Shape of Things to Come: The Ultimate Revolution (1933) novel

Experiment in Autobiography: Discoveries and Conclusions of a Very Ordinary Brain (Since 1866) (1934) nonfiction

The Anatomy of Frustration: A Modern Synthesis (1936) nonfiction

The Croquet Player: A Story (1936) novel

Star Begotten: A Biological Fantasia (1937) novel

Brynhild (1937) novel

The Camford Visitation (1937) novel

Apropos of Dolores (1938) novel

World Brain (1938) nonfiction

The Brothers: A Story (1938) novel

The Holy Terror (1939) novel

The Fate of Man: An Unemotional Statement of the Things That Are Happening to Him Now, and of the Immediate Possibilities Confronting Him (1939) nonfiction

Babes in the Darkling Wood (1940) novel
All Aboard for Ararat (1940) novel
You Can't Be Too Careful: A Sample of Life, 1901–1951
    (1941) novel
Crux Ansata: An Indictment of the Roman Catholic Church
    (1943) nonfiction
*'42 to '44: A Contemporary Memoir upon Human Be-
    havior During the Crisis of the World Revolution*
    (1944) nonfiction
Mind at the End of Its Tether (1945) nonfiction

BOOKS FOR FURTHER READING

Bergonzi, Bernard. *The Early H. G. Wells: A Study of the
    Scientific Romances*. Manchester: Manchester Uni-
    versity Press, 1961.

Coren, Michael. *The Invisible Man: The Life and Liber-
    ties of H. G. Wells*. London: Bloomsbury, 1993.

Delbanco, Nicholas. *Group Portrait: Joseph Conrad, Ste-
    phen Crane, Ford Madox Ford, Henry James, and H. G.
    Wells*. New York: Morrow, 1982.

Dickson, Lovat. *H. G. Wells: His Turbulent Life and Times*.
    New York: Atheneum, 1969.

Foot, Michael. *H. G.: The History of Mr. Wells*. London:
    Doubleday, 1995.

Hammond, John R. *H. G. Wells and the Modern Novel*.
    Basingstoke, Hampshire, England: Macmillan, 1988.

Huntington, John. *Critical Essays on H. G. Wells*. Bos-
    ton: G. K. Hall, 1991.

——, ed. *The Logic of Fantasy: H. G. Wells and Science
    Fiction*. New York: Columbia University Press, 1982.

James, Simon J. *Maps of Utopia: H. G. Wells, Modernity
    and the End of Culture*. Oxford: Oxford University
    Press, 2012.

MacKenzie, Norman and Jeanne. *The Life of H. G. Wells*.
    Rev. ed. London: Hogarth, 1987.

McConnell, Frank D. *The Science Fiction of H. G. Wells*.
    Oxford: Oxford University Press, 1981.

McLean, Steven. *The Early Fiction of H. G. Wells: Fantasies of Science.* New York: Palgrave Macmillan, 2009.

Parrinder, Patrick. *H. G. Wells.* Edinburgh, Scotland, and London: Oliver and Boyd, 1970.

——, ed. *H. G. Wells: The Critical Heritage.* London: Routledge and Kegan Paul, 1972.

——. *Shadows of the Future: H. G. Wells, Science Fiction, and Prophecy.* Liverpool: Liverpool University Press, 1995.

Partington, John S. *Building Cosmopolis: The Political Thought of H. G. Wells.* Aldershot: Ashgate Publishing Limited, 2003.

Scheick, William J. *H. G. Wells: A Reference Guide.* Boston: G.K. Hall, 1988.

——. *The Critical Response to H. G. Wells.* Westport, CT: Greenwood Press, 1995.

Sherborne, Michael. *H. G. Wells: Another Kind of Life.* London: Peter Owen, 2010.

Slusser, George, Patrick Parrinder, and Danièle Chatelain, eds. *H. G. Wells's Perennial Time Machine: Selected Essays from the Centenary Conference "The Time Machine: Present, Past, and Future."* Athens: University of Georgia Press, 2001.

Smith, David C., ed. *The Correspondence of H. G. Wells.* 4 vols. London: Pickering and Chatto, 1998.

——. *H. G. Wells: Desperately Mortal: A Biography.* New Haven, CT: Yale University Press, 1986.

Wagar, W. Warren. *H. G. Wells and the World State.* New Haven, CT: Yale University Press, 1961.

Wells, G. P., ed. *H. G. Wells in Love: Postscript to an Experiment in Autobiography.* Boston: Little, Brown, 1984.

READ THE TOP 20
SIGNET CLASSICS

1984 BY GEORGE ORWELL

ANIMAL FARM BY GEORGE ORWELL

NARRATIVE OF THE LIFE OF FREDERICK DOUGLASS
    BY FREDERICK DOUGLASS

THE INFERNO BY DANTE

ROMEO AND JULIET BY WILLIAM SHAKESPEARE

WHY WE CAN'T WAIT BY DR. MARTIN LUTHER KING, JR.

NECTAR IN A SIEVE BY KAMALA MARKANDAYA

FRANKENSTEIN BY MARY SHELLEY

BEOWULF TRANSLATED BY BURTON RAFFEL

HAMLET BY WILLIAM SHAKESPEARE

THE FEDERALIST PAPERS BY ALEXANDER HAMILTON

THE ODYSSEY BY HOMER

MACBETH BY WILLIAM SHAKESPEARE

CRIME AND PUNISHMENT BY FYODOR DOSTOYEVSKY

THE HOUND OF THE BASKERVILLES
    BY SIR ARTHUR CONAN DOYLE

THE SCARLET LETTER BY NATHANIEL HAWTHORNE

DR. JEKYLL AND MR. HYDE BY ROBERT L. STEVENSON

A MIDSUMMER NIGHT'S DREAM BY WILLIAM SHAKESPEARE

THE CLASSIC SLAVE NARRATIVES BY HENRY L. GATES

A TALE OF TWO CITIES BY CHARLES DICKENS

PENGUIN.COM
FACEBOOK.COM/SIGNETCLASSIC